MCA
J

Nanny X

Madelyn Rosenberg

illustrations by Karen Donnelly

Holiday House / New York

Library of Congress Cataloging-in-Publication data
Rosenberg, Madelyn, 1966–
Nanny X / by Madelyn Rosenberg. — First edition.
pages cm
Summary: Ten-year-old Alison and eight-year-old Jake discover that their nanny is
working undercover to catch criminals.
ISBN 978-0-8234-3166-3 (hardcover : alk. paper) [1. Nannies—Fiction.
2. Brothers and sisters—Fiction. 3. Undercover operations—Fiction.]
I. Title.
PZ7.R71897Nan 2014
[Fic]—dc23
2013045487

For Andrew, Melanie and Jules

Acknowledgements

HQ: Mary Cash and everyone at Holiday House

The Usual Suspects: Anamaria Anderson, Tom Angleberger, Cece Bell, Mary Crockett, Marfé Ferguson Delano, Moira Rose Donohue, Marty Rhodes Figley, Anna Hebner, Carla Heymsfeld, Jacqueline Jules, Liz Macklin, Suzy McIntire, Laura Murray, Wendy Shang, Rachael Walker, the Deemers, the Lazorchaks, the Rosenbergs, the Striers, the Briers, the A-Team, the Girls and the Nuts.

The Unusual Suspects: Kathryn Erskine, Laurel Snyder, Margie Myers-Culver, Jama Rattigan, Tamson Weston, Dana Cann, Jim Beane, Jim Mathews, Catherine Bell, Kathleen Wheaton, Carmelinda Blagg and Karen Donnelly.

Secret Agents: Susan Cohen and Brianne Johnson.

Special Agents: Graham and Karina Lazorchak, Cole Snavely and Ethan Burka.

Special Ops: Butch Lazorchak and everyone who taste-tested the coconut smoothies and peanut butter and anchovy sandwiches.

Contents

1. Alison

Nanny X = Spooky

Someone pounded on our front door at 7:29 A.M.

I didn't answer, even though it would have been the helpful thing to do. My brother, Jake, didn't answer, either, but not because he wasn't being helpful; he'd just invented a game called Breakfast Cereal Baseball and he had a batter up. My father didn't answer the door because he hadn't had enough coffee yet. Eliza didn't answer it because she's not even two, and Yeti didn't answer it because he's a dog. Also, my parents had locked him in my bedroom.

"Isn't somebody going to get that?" my mother called from upstairs. I didn't move. Jake flicked a Honey Berry Bomb across the table. It hit me in the neck.

"I didn't mean to," he said before I could call him a doofus. "Guess that's an out."

Thud. Thud. Thud. The knocks came louder this time, like somebody shouting at us in Morse code. Then came the sound of my mother clomping down the stairs. You could tell it had been a long time since she'd worn high heels.

We heard the front door open, then voices.

"Kids? Richard?" my mother called. She sounded chirpy, like when she told us how much fun it would be to clean the toilets.

"Ahm!" yelled Eliza as my dad lifted her up.

"Come on, team," he said. "You have a date with destiny." Jake popped one last Berry Bomb into his mouth as we followed my dad to the front door.

"Kids," my mother said again. She sounded even chirpier, like she was going to lift up a sheet and reveal a shiny silver bicycle. Only she didn't have a sheet. And she didn't have a bicycle.

What she had was a woman with silver-gray hair, a straw gardening hat with pink flowers, and no smile. She wore a black motorcycle jacket and a pair of mirrored sunglasses. She smelled like a combination of chicken soup and motor oil, and it looked like she had borrowed her shoes from a Pilgrim.

"This is your new nanny!" my mother said. I could hear the *ta-da* in her voice, but I didn't feel like I'd won anything.

"Pleased to meet you," Jake said, sticking out his hand like he was trying to win the "Most Polite Kid of the Year" award. The nanny shook it.

I clamped my lips together so the word "hello" could not get through them. The nanny stood back and studied us through her sunglasses, though with the reflection it was hard to tell where her eyes were really looking. All I could see was my own face, also not smiling, staring back at her.

"Yes," she told my mother. "Yes, I think they'll do."

Do? I thought. *Do what?*

"Allow me to introduce myself," the nanny continued, getting down to business. "I am Nanny X."

This time I did open my mouth. "That's weird," I said.

"*Alison Pringle*," said my mother.

"But X isn't even a *real name*!" I pointed out.

"It is my *chosen* name," said Nanny X. She spoke fast, like someone was timing her. "My given name is long and boring, and I've always felt sorry for the letter X. There aren't enough words that begin with X."

I had to admit she was right. Eliza has about a thousand alphabet books, and in every single one, X stands for xylophone.

"Not many names begin with Z, either," said Jake. He is obsessed with initials.

Nanny X smiled for the first time. Her face didn't look half bad that way. "Ah, but your middle name begins with Z," she said. "Zachary, am I right?" My mother must have told her a lot about us, if she knew Jake's middle name. My middle name is Theresa, but the nanny didn't mention it.

"I think I should stick with X," the nanny said.

"Not many names begin with Y," said Jake. I wondered if he was going to go through the whole alphabet.

"But you have a dog, do you not?" Nanny X turned toward my father, who was still holding Eliza. "Yeti? How are his fleas?"

"His fleas are much better, thank you," my father said. He cleared his throat after he talked, instead of before.

Yeti whimpered from my bedroom. My parents had put him there so he wouldn't pounce on the nanny as soon as she came through the door.

"Well," the nanny said. "I can stand here like a schlump or I can make your lunches. To the kitchen! Away!" She snatched Eliza out of my father's arms and walked toward the kitchen like she owned the place. Her mirrored glasses were still perched on her nose. Then she paused and turned. "Please note, Alison, that your lunch today will not contain any bubble gum."

I could feel my face go red, like the time I tripped getting off the school bus and landed in dog poop. *She knew!* Somehow Nanny X knew that I had secretly chewed gum in Ms. Bertram's class on Friday. She probably knew that I'd gotten caught and had to spend the rest of the day with gum on my nose. I hadn't told my parents about it, or even my little brother. And why did a nanny know about Yeti's fleas? Who mentions fleas during a nanny interview? Especially if you're trying to get the nanny to *take* the job? Maybe Nanny X could read minds.

My dad took another gulp of coffee and hurried off to his job at the Museum of Natural History. My mother went to grab her briefcase for her new job as a lawyer. I followed her.

"Well, what do you think?" she asked.

"She dresses funny," I said.

"Of course she does; she's from New York."

"And she's spooky," I said.

"Spooky how?"

"Knowing about Yeti's fleas, and . . . other stuff."

"Look, I know you're still angry, Alison, but this is okay, isn't it? Me going back to work? Of course the biggest change is for Eliza. You and Jake will be in school all day. Anyway, you'll like Nanny X. It's just for a few weeks, until we find a permanent nanny. But the agency said she was special."

My mother was so busy getting ready for work, she didn't even notice that I didn't answer her. In the kitchen she gave the nanny a million last-minute instructions.

Then she kissed all of us (except Nanny X). "Wish me luck," she said. We did, and she left for stupid old Mathers and Mathers, where she was going to work even though she was not a Mathers.

Nanny X was officially in charge.

2. Jake

Nanny X Strikes Out

The sign on my sister's door says Keep Out, and I am pretty sure she has the exact same sign hanging on her brain, because she acts like she doesn't want anyone in there. Especially "pesky little brothers." I am not pesky and I am almost as tall as she is, but she ignores me when I say that. My friend Ethan says that this is unsurprising because fifth grade is the year older sisters turn snotty. But Ali started off the year being kind of nice. It wasn't until our mom started talking about the nanny thing that she turned into a Super Snot, which is what I decided to call her. But not out loud. I just call her that in the keep-out part of my own brain. Sometimes I just use initials.

I decided that if Ali was going to ignore everything I say, then I could ignore the things she says. Like "keep out." Anyway, I wasn't really breaking her privacy, because Ali wasn't even in her room, plus, it's a stupid sign. Plus, I was *mostly* keeping out. I just wanted to set Yeti free.

I cracked her door open. *Swoosh.* Yeti shot right out of

there. He didn't stop to lick my hand, but I could tell he was glad that I'd taken care of things.

"Arf-arf-arf-arf-arf." Yeti ran downstairs, straight for the kitchen and probably straight for Nanny X. He always jumps on strangers, and Nanny X was a pretty strange stranger—stranger than Mr. Frank, the mailman. Yeti always barks at Mr. Frank, who shouldn't even be a stranger by now because he's been coming to our house almost every day for five years.

Yeti is named after the abominable snowman. He looks kind of like a polar bear, except he's not as big. I read in *Fantastically Freaky Animal Facts* that even though polar bears look white, their fur is *translucent*. Yeti's fur is white. I wished he could be in charge of us, like that dog in Peter Pan. Then the Super Snot could go back to acting the way she did in the good old days. If the new nanny was unconscious in the kitchen because Yeti jumped on her, maybe he'd get the chance to take over.

But Nanny X was not lying on the floor. When I got to the kitchen, she was standing up. She had taken off her sunglasses, and she was staring right into Yeti's eyes. I didn't see laser beams, but Yeti stared back as if Nanny X was controlling him with her mind. *If she looks away*, I thought, *he'll jump on her for sure.* But when she looked at me, Yeti kept looking at *her*, like she was the best thing since bacon-flavored dog treats.

"Why don't you get in a few minutes for your reading log before school?" Nanny X said. She didn't say anything about mind control or about the Honey Berry Bombs on the floor. I thought maybe she was good at ignoring things, too. "Try the sports section," she added. "It counts."

I was so happy that reading about the Nationals game counted for my reading log that I didn't stop to wonder how she knew I had a reading log in the first place. I took the paper and went into the living room. I looked out the window, hoping to see a motorcycle that matched Nanny X's jacket, maybe with a sidecar and some extra helmets or something. But I just saw a regular, boring minivan. Rats. I looked at the paper. Rats again—the Nats lost. But then my eyes found something that had nothing to do with the Nationals but still had lots to do with me.

New Factory May Replace Old Park

LOVETT—Rawlings Park, a favorite among Lovett youth, will close if the mayor has his way. The scenic park, which features a playground, a baseball diamond, and tall oaks, is in what Mayor John Osbourne calls a "prime business location." Osbourne confirmed that the county is considering selling the land to make way for a factory. "It's going to be big, big, big," he said. A public meeting will be held in the park today at 2 p.m., in advance of the Lovett Planning Commission meeting.

"They can't do that." I slammed the paper down like my dad does when he doesn't agree with something.

"What are you even talking about?" I hadn't heard my sister come into the living room, but there she was, grabbing the newspaper away from me without even asking.

"The mayor closing the park," I said. In my head I added: *Super Snot.*

My baseball team practices at that park. Half of our games are there. Plus, the playground has a blue slide that looks like an intestine. According to *Fantastically Freaky Facts about the Human Body*, the small intestine is about twenty feet long, but the large intestine is only five feet long. It's wider, which is how it got its name.

"Maybe I could handcuff myself to home plate," I said.

"There's no place to attach the handcuffs," Ali said.

"I could lie down on top of it." I pictured myself on the news, surrounded by a bunch of construction dudes who couldn't turn on their bulldozers because of me.

"Two minutes until the bus," Nanny X called. "Jake, Brush your teeth."

"I already did," I called back.

"Yes, but you forgot your tongue," she said. I went to brush again while Ali finished reading the article.

On the way to the bus, my Super Snot sister walked the length of a small intestine in front of the rest of us. Yeti trotted beside me with half a Honey Berry Bomb on his lip, which meant that he'd helped clean up the kitchen. Actually, "trotted" is not the right word; Nanny X was too slow for trotting. She didn't look like she could pitch, either, which is something I'd been hoping I would get in a new nanny. But between staying on her feet when Yeti jumped on her and figuring out that the sports section counted on my reading log, which always came back marked "More variety, please," her batting average seemed okay.

It dropped at lunch.

Dead fish is not the smell you want coming out of your lunch box, but it was coming out of mine. Nanny X had packed me a peanut butter and anchovy sandwich. The smell was so bad I couldn't get past it to see if she had packed me anything else. The smell was so bad Ethan moved to the peanut-free table to get away from me. I threw the sandwich in the trash, but the smell did not go in the trash with it. It *lingered*, which is one of my reading connection words. The definition is: when a dead-fermented-fishy smell won't go away and you have to bury your lunch box.

Nanny X just struck out, I thought. But I found out later that the game hadn't started yet.

3. Alison

Nanny X Pitches

So to answer my mother's question: It was not okay.

My mother going back to work was not okay.

My lunch was not okay.

The mayor closing the park was not okay.

And being taken care of by an unsmiling nanny who knew way too much about us was not okay, either. I hoped she didn't go snooping around my bedroom while I was stuck in the classroom, listening to Ms. Bertram teach us the names for different foods in Spanish. Her idea of the day was to have us draw pictures of food with their proper Spanish names, and then trade them with friends, like Yu-Gi-Oh cards.

I started by drawing a pack of gum, *chicle*, for my friend Ellie, who had to spend the day with *chicle* on her nose. I knew how she felt, which is why I gave her the drawing.

Ellie smiled. Ms. Bertram did not. "Señorita Pringle," she said. She only uses our last names during Spanish, which I'm good at because I can roll my R's. Most of the kids just make gargling noises in their throats. "Do we swallow gum? No. Therefore I do not count it as a food source. Make another choice."

I looked around to make sure Nanny X hadn't suddenly appeared outside the window and overheard all of this, but all I could see was the green field where we had recess and, beyond that, a creek where we collected specimens to look at under the microscope. I took out another piece of paper and drew a fish, *un pescado*. Nobody wanted to trade for it, probably because they'd smelled my lunch. Or possibly because I'd made the fish look as angry as I felt. Finally I traded it to my friend Stinky Malloy for a friendly-looking carrot, *una zanahoria*.

"As long as it isn't lentils, I'll take it," he said. Stinky has had the same nanny, Boris, since he was two or three years old. Except for an obsession with lentils, Boris actually seemed kind of cool. He also had a real name, unlike another nanny I knew.

The clock ticked toward early release. To make the time go faster, I practiced tying knots in my shoelaces with a pencil. I've been trying to learn different ones, like the figure eight and the cow hitch. It would help if I decided to try mountain climbing or cattle rustling, but mostly, tying knots kept me from biting my fingernails. I'd done pretty well with not biting them this week, until the new nanny showed up. By lunch I'd chewed off every fingernail except for my right thumb and left pinky.

My brother sat diagonally across from me on the bus on the way home.

"Anchovies," was the first thing he said.

"You could have tried scraping them off," said Stinky,

who sat behind me. He was wearing his yellow bus-patrol belt.

"You can't scrape them off," said Jake. "They infect everything."

Like Nanny X's brain, I thought. I hoped Eliza was okay.

Stinky moved up a few seats to remind Rebecca Gin, who is in kindergarten, to get off at her stop. When he came back he said: "I have to make my own lunch, to guard against the lentils. You'll probably have to do the same thing. Is she nice, at least?"

"She doesn't smile much," Jake answered. "I thought nannies were supposed to smile. Mary Poppins did."

"Not always," I said.

We'd seen *Mary Poppins* four times in the past two weeks. It was part of my mother's plan to brainwash us into thinking it was okay for her to hire a nanny and go back to being a lawyer. The brainwashing didn't work. The only thing that was different was that now my dad hummed that "Chim Chim Cher-ee" song all of the time.

"Are you going to the park later?" Stinky asked me, changing the subject. My heart got kind of fluttery, even though I absolutely did not have a crush on Stinky. "There's a big meeting this afternoon," he added. "If we hurry, we can make it." In addition to being a member of the bus patrol, Stinky was president of the Watson Elementary Green Team, so it made sense that he'd be interested in what happened to the park.

"They can't put a factory there," I said. I was glad Jake had finally read something besides his Fantastically Freaky books.

"We have to fight to save it," Stinky agreed, standing up for his stop. "This is our future." I was pretty sure he meant "our" as in "our planet" and not "our" as in "Stinky and Ali." But going to the park seemed like something we should do.

"I'll be there," I said.

"If we can talk the nanny into it," Jake butted in.

Our stop was next. The bus doors made a gassy sound as Miss Pat opened them. Nanny X was waiting, holding Eliza, who was wearing a little dress with cherries on it that were even redder than her hair. She was smiling, which I guessed meant that her diaper was clean and that she hadn't eaten ground-up anchovies for lunch. Yeti wagged his tail. The nanny had on her hat and her motorcycle jacket and those mirrored glasses again.

"How was your day?" the nanny asked as we dumped our backpacks in Eliza's stroller. Eliza wasn't using it. "Lunch was good, I hope?" Nanny X's mouth made a straight line, like a zipper. I couldn't tell if she was serious or if the anchovies had been her idea of a joke, or a test—or, like Stinky said, a way to get us to make our own lunches.

"Actually—" I began, but the nanny interrupted.

"Protein. Brain food. A winning combination. And we need our brains today. Push the stroller, Jake. We're off to the park."

As much as I wanted to go to the park—I was glad I didn't have to convince her, after all—I was hoping to get something to eat first. "What about our snack?" I said.

"Here." Nanny X reached into a steel-gray diaper bag that matched her hair, and pulled out an apple for each of us. She tossed them one at a time.

"You can pitch!" Jake crowed. He looked ready to forgive the anchovies.

"I was the MVP of the South Brooklyn girls softball team," Nanny X said. She didn't mention what year. "Now come. We have a meeting to go to."

"The save-the-park meeting?" It was almost as if she'd overheard our conversation with Stinky. Or maybe she'd just heard Jake and me that morning, in the living room.

"I believe both sides will be represented, but yes."

"How did you know about it?" I said. If I could get her to admit to eavesdropping, maybe my mother would decide that leaving us with a nanny was a big mistake. My mother hates eavesdropping.

"It's my business to know," Nanny X said. "Yours, too, I should think." She concentrated hard on her walking.

When we got to the park, it seemed like a lot of people had made it their business to know. Or maybe everyone who lives near Washington, D.C., just likes to protest. The place was packed, and everyone had signs. Be Green Not Mean. Use Space with Grace. On the other side of the park, more people carried signs. Only these signs said things like Let Us Grow and More Dollars Makes Sense! I didn't see Stinky anywhere.

Nanny X walked through the signs like they were just trees and not a bunch of angry parents and businesspeople and kids. She spread out a blue sheet that almost matched the sky, and plunked my sister in the middle of it. "Homework," she said to me and Jake. "Chop-chop." She pulled two pencils out of the diaper bag and blew on the tips. "By my count you have exactly ten minutes until something happens. That's enough time to finish your math."

"How did you know we have math homework?" I asked Nanny X.

"Children always have math homework," she said. "And I know a lot of things."

"What's the volume of this prism?" I asked.

"Regular or irregular?" She glanced at my paper.

"Regular."

"To answer that would be irresponsible. That's your homework, not mine."

Nanny X was like a Magic 8 Ball; half of her answers weren't even answers. But I had one more question.

"Who's going to save the park?" I asked.

Nanny X took off her sunglasses and looked at me with eyes that were the color of a thunderstorm. This time she answered directly.

"We are," she said.

4. Jake

Nanny X Gets Weirder

The only thing I've ever saved before is a baby rabbit when Yeti caught one in the backyard, and I am pretty sure that saving a park is not the same thing as saving a rabbit. You can't feed a park milk from an eyedropper. You can't deliver it to the animal rescue lady. Maybe Nanny X would teach me how to do mind control, like she used on Yeti, so I could use it on the mayor and convince him to leave our park alone.

I pulled out a piece of notebook paper and made my own sign: Baseball Is a Diamond. I drew bases with some lines coming out from them, so it looked like they were all glowy.

Nanny X looked at her watch. "Five. Four. Three. Two. Now."

At "now," a lady got up onto the stage. She had glasses, plus hair that went all the way down to her butt, and she held up a Be Green Not Mean sign. I wondered if I could count reading those signs for my reading log, too.

"Friends," Mrs. Green-Not-Mean said into a megaphone. "We are here because it has come to our attention that the mayor is attempting to rush through this park's destruction, and we thought if you could just see the park, just see our children at play, you would realize that we do not need a factory here."

"*What if I don't have any children?*" a man yelled. He didn't raise his hand or anything.

Mrs. Green-Not-Mean's voice got kind of quavery. "Lovett's children belong to all of us," she said. "And I am here to tell you that they do not need another fast-food restaurant, they do not need another warehouse. I beg you, look at the children and you will see that this is what they— what *we*—really need." She spread her arms and looked at the trees like she wanted to hug them. I moved a little behind Nanny X in case she decided that she wanted to hug me, too, since I was one of Lovett's children.

Half of the people in the audience clapped. The lady wiped her eyes and sat back down.

"Friends." A man took out a megaphone that was like the lady's, only bigger. He had a shiny spot on his head where hair used to be. "My name is Rufus Strathmore, chairman of the Lovett Chamber of Commerce." He waited for people to clap. "How do you think we support the many fine things our city has? Business. What do we need? Business. Because business means jobs, and that is what will help our children most."

Then people started yelling, "What kind of jobs?" And everyone held up their signs, including me. I saw Stinky Malloy standing near the front. His sign was on actual poster board, not notebook paper, and it said Slides Are Cool. That's what he started chanting. Then a bunch more people joined in. "Slides are cool! Slides are cool!" Ali and I chanted, too, even though I would have said the slide was cooler than just the regular kind of cool. It was dry-ice cool! It was frozen-tundra cool! Plus, I would have worked in something about the ball field. And intestines.

The Green-Not-Mean lady got back onstage. "*Slides are cool!*" she yelled.

"Excuse me, madam, but you know nothing about—"

"*Slides are cool!*"

"This land will bring industry to the heart of our city," said Rufus Strathmore.

"*This land is already in use!*" shouted Mrs. Green-Not-Mean. Her voice got really high on the last word, like those opera singers who can shatter glass. Mr. Strathmore and Mrs. Green-Not-Mean started screaming at each other without even using their megaphones. The mayor jumped onstage and stood between them, like he was trying to break it up, even though we all knew whose side he was really on.

Nanny X pulled a pair of binoculars from the diaper bag. She wasn't watching the stage anymore, though. She was watching the crowd.

I watched the stage, which is why I saw the big, brown rock flying right toward it. *Pow.* It hit the mayor in the head.

"Help him!" someone yelled. "Help the mayor! He's been hit."

Mr. Strathmore and Mrs. Green-Not-Mean were quiet for about four seconds while they looked at the mayor, who was all slumpy in the middle of the platform. Then they started yelling again.

"Is there a doctor in the park?"

"What kind of stunt is this?"

"Call 911."

"Your people know all about stunts."

I wondered if Nanny X was going to take us home. That's what happens whenever my mom sees grown-ups misbehaving. But Nanny X did not take us home. Instead, she took a diaper out of the diaper bag. I thought she was going to change Eliza, and Eliza must have thought the same thing, because she rolled onto her back and stuck her legs up in the air and wiggled them. But Nanny X took the diaper and walked over to one side of a big tree. She unfolded the diaper and held it up to her face. Her lips moved, like she was asking the diaper if it was having a nice day. If Nanny X expected that diaper to talk back to her, then Ali and I had a bigger problem than the mayor turning our park into a factory.

5. Alison

Nanny X Asks the Questions

Something told me that even in New York, nobody talked to diapers. Maybe Nanny X was just *smelling* the diaper to make sure it was clean. And her lips were moving because . . . that helped her smell better? But I heard her voice.

"Yes," she told the diaper. "I quite agree. It's started. Right. I'm on it." She crumpled up the diaper and started back toward us.

"Should we call Mom?" Jake asked. He didn't bother to whisper, and I knew what he was thinking. He was thinking that when the grown-up who's supposed to be taking care of you starts talking to diapers, it's time to go find another grown-up.

But even with her strange clothes, and even with her definitely knowing about Yeti's fleas and her probably knowing about Ms. Bertram and the gum—even with her general spookiness—Nanny X seemed like she was only partly nuts. Not totally.

"May I join your conversation?" she said.

"I thought you were already having your own conversation." I knew that wasn't exactly the way to talk to a grown-up. But I thought it might be the way to talk to a grown-up who talked to diapers. Besides, somebody had to be in charge; I was the oldest.

Nanny X moved her glasses down her nose and looked at me over the rims. I looked back, not quite as pleasantly.

"Fine," Nanny X said. "Though I must say I was rather counting on your cooperation. This is a disappointment."

If there's one thing I hate, it's when grown-ups tell you they're "disappointed." I decided to put everything out in the open. "Did we just see you talking to a diaper?" I didn't add "weirdo" at the end of my question. See? I *can* be polite.

"No," said Nanny X. "You did not."

"Uh, excuse me," I said, polite again. "But yes we did."

"Ah," Nanny X said. "You thought you did. But you see, children, I was not talking *to* the diaper. I was talking *through* it. I'll ex—"

"*We've found the culprit*," Police Chief Grummel announced from the stage. Everyone stopped talking.

"*Let me repeat*," said the chief, even though we all heard him the first time. "*We have found the culprit*."

Two more police officers rushed to the platform. They had their "culprit" by the collar. He was skinny, with longish dark hair, and he was holding a Slides Are Cool sign. It only took us two seconds to realize that who they had was Stinky Malloy. That seemed even crazier than Nanny X talking to diapers.

The mayor, who was lying on a stretcher about to be carried away, looked up at Stinky. "Book him," he said.

Stinky Malloy! He turned in quarters when he found them on the playground. It's true, he was concerned about the environment, and there were probably a lot of things he'd do to keep a factory from being plunked in the middle of Lovett. But he wouldn't hurt anybody. I was sure about that.

"*I didn't do it!*" yelled Stinky.

"*My head!*" yelled the mayor.

"I didn't do it!" Stinky told the police officers, who completely ignored him. Then Stinky saw us.

"Ali! Jake!" he said. "Tell them it wasn't me."

"It wasn't him," I said, moving forward. "You've got to listen. Please. It wasn't him."

"If it wasn't you," said Chief Grummel, who was listening now that Stinky was talking to somebody else, "then what's this?" He held up a round rock, about the size of a potato—the boiled kind, not the baking kind.

"I didn't throw that," Stinky said. "I was just holding it. You found it in my *hand*."

"Where there's smoke, there's fire," the chief said. "Get me a stick; I want to roast a hot dog."

"But it's true," Stinky said. "I picked it up because I thought it might be a geode."

"Throwing rocks at the mayor is a criminal offense," said the chief. "You have the right to remain silent, and we have the right to take you to the police station."

"My mother's going to kill me," said Stinky Malloy.

"You see," said the chief. "Even his mother thinks he's guilty."

"You've made a mistake," I said. "You can't arrest a kid."

"Watch me," said Chief Grummel. He started to lead Stinky away.

"Stinky didn't do it," I told Nanny X. "I know he didn't."

"Tell me about him," she said.

I looked at Nanny X again, the nanny who had known us for only a few hours but who knew about Ms. Bertram and gum and a billion other things she shouldn't know.

The nanny who was ready to save the park. The nanny who dressed funny and talked to diapers. She wasn't my first choice, but there was no one else to tell. So I told her.

Stinky Malloy lived over on Hummel Street. He was in my grade at Watson Elementary, but he looked older because he kept having growth spurts. Sometimes you couldn't see his eyes because his bangs needed cutting.

I told her that everyone in our school knew Stinky because when he was in third grade he signed up our class to collect litter along Main Street. Only none of the parents wanted their children picking up litter along Main Street because of the traffic. So then the parents had to pick up all of the litter themselves.

The other reason Stinky Malloy was famous was because last summer he was walking his dog, Edgar, when Edgar discovered a skunk. The skunk got mad and sprayed like crazy. Edgar got out of the way, but Stinky didn't. He was so stinky after that skunk, even his freckles smelled bad. Everyone kept calling him "Stinky" even after he'd had three baths and washed his hair with tomato juice. His real name was Daniel. That was the name the police officers would probably book him under. Also he was the most honest kid I knew.

"He has a nanny named Boris," I told Nanny X. Boris. *He* could fix things. I looked around, but I didn't see him anywhere, and Boris is hard to miss; he's at least six foot three. "They eat a lot of lentils," I added.

"Ali!" Stinky called as Chief Grummel opened the door to the squad car. "Find Boris and tell him where I am. Please?" I looked at Nanny X. She nodded, just once.

"Don't worry," I called. "We'll help you."

Now we were supposed to save more than the park. Now we were supposed to save Stinky Malloy.

6. Jake

Nanny X Drops a Bomb

I've never seen anybody taken to jail in real life before. They put Stinky in handcuffs, just like they do on TV. Plus, they made him sit in the back of the police car behind that cage thing, which made it look like he was *already* in jail.

I started to say something to Ali, but even her hair looked dark and angry, so I tugged on Nanny X's motorcycle jacket instead. "Now what?" I said.

"You made a promise to Daniel, correct?" It took me a second to remember that Daniel was really Stinky.

"We're supposed to find Boris," I said.

"Daniel will get a phone call, once he reaches police headquarters, but in this case I think it would be best if his family had a head start. I will contact the nanny."

"You don't even know Boris's last name," Ali said, but Nanny X walked away from us and pulled out that diaper again. I wondered if she talked to bananas, too. Or toilets.

Ali picked up Eliza. What if the police came back and took us away, too, because we were friends with Stinky? What if they thought we were all in on it?

When Nanny X came back, she announced: "I contacted Boris. You will be happy to know that he is already en route to the station, along with Daniel's mother."

"Contacted him *how*?" Ali said. "With that diaper? With your hat?"

"Yeah," I said. "How?"

"We are wasting time," Nanny X said. "We should be looking for clues."

"Do we get any clues about you?" Ali asked, not politely, but not impolitely, either. "Like are you even a real nanny?" Except for that last part. Ali made her eyes small and crossed her arms. "What were you doing with that diaper? How did you know about Yeti's fleas?"

Nanny X almost smiled. "You'd make a good lawyer, Alison," she said. "Speaking of lawyers—"

"Mom!" I shouted. "Our mom's a lawyer! She can get Stinky out of jail."

"She's an *immigration* lawyer," Ali said in her S.S. voice. "Not a get-Stinky-out-of-jail lawyer."

"So?" I said. "She's a *good* lawyer." Maybe she hadn't been doing it much lately, but she could help Stinky. I knew she could.

"Call her," Nanny X said. I waited for her to give me the diaper, which would have been zero help and 100 percent gross, but she handed me an actual cell phone. I dialed my mom's new number, which she made us memorize in case of emergencies. I thought about telling my mom about our nanny talking to the diaper, but it wasn't really dangerous, and if I did that, she might forget about helping Stinky, so I just told her the Stinky part.

"Are you sure?" she said. "Are you sure that's what happened?"

I handed the phone to Nanny X. "That's what happened," she told my mother. "Jake Z gave you a very precise account." She looked like she wanted to say something else, but she didn't. I put the phone back against my ear.

"They can't do that," Mom said. "In a squad car? For Pete's sake. I'll make some calls. Try not to worry, Jakey, okay? I know it's upsetting, but try to focus on something else. Are you getting along with your sisters?"

She said sisters, meaning both of them, but I knew which one she really meant. "Sure," I said.

"You take care of each other," she said.

"We will." I handed the phone back to Nanny X. "She's making some calls," I said.

"Good," she said. "Now let's get to work. Search the trees. Search the bushes. Search everywhere."

"What are we looking for?"

"Well, for one thing, we're looking for whatever *really* hit the mayor," said Nanny X. "Because something tells me it wasn't that rock your friend Daniel was carrying. And as always, we are seeking anything out of the ordinary. You should always be alert for anything out of the ordinary."

I wasn't sure what we would find that was out of the ordinary (besides Nanny X), but I started looking around, plus, so did Yeti. He pricked up his ears and sniffed the ground, as if he understood exactly what Nanny X was telling us to do.

Ali didn't search with us. She just stood there with her arms crossed, glaring at Nanny X.

"Yes?" Nanny X said.

"I want to know what's going on."

"So do I," said Nanny X.

"No," Ali said. "I mean I want to know what's going on about *you*."

Nanny X raised an eyebrow over her sunglasses. Ali raised one, too.

"I will tell you," Nanny X said finally, "if you can promise not to tell anyone else. And only because we must work together quickly if we're going to help Daniel, this park, and this town."

"I promise," I said.

"I need to hear it first," said Ali. Nanny X took off her sunglasses. Then she spoke, more slowly than she'd spoken all day.

"What does the word 'NAP' mean to you?"

"We don't take naps anymore," I said. "Only Eliza does."

"Not 'nap'" said Nanny X. She loaded our backpacks into the bottom part of Eliza's stroller and strapped Eliza into the seat part. "*NAP*. N.A.P."

"Oh!" I said. "That's different."

Washington, D.C., is full of agencies with initials. I had a lot of them memorized, like NDIIPP (National Digital Information Infrastructure Preservation Program) and NHDSC (National Hot Dog and Sausage Council). When I came across initials I didn't recognize, I liked to guess what they stood for before I found out for real. I'd seen NAP in the news a few times: NAP Nabs Crime Ring; NAP Saves Prime Minister. They were my favorite kind of initials, because they were an acronym, which meant you could put them together and make a word. But for some weirdo reason, I'd never been able to learn what the initials stood for. The news never said, plus I'd checked the phone book, plus the Internet. Nothing.

But Nanny X knew.

"It's a secret organization," she explained. "Classified. For most of the world, NAP is all they need to know. But it actually stands for Nanny Action Patrol."

Ali made a snorting sound, like a horse with a dragonfly up its nose. I didn't snort. I knew what NAP could do. If our nanny was a member of NAP, it didn't matter if she talked to diapers or even if she put anchovies in our lunch boxes. If our nanny was a member of NAP, she was *tundra* cool. Plus, things were about to become very un-boring.

"I've been a member of NAP for three years," our nanny said, "ever since I retired from another undercover organization whose initials I'm not at liberty to share." She took off her hat and fanned herself. "Our headquarters was not too far from here, but when I reached retirement age they told me to go back to New York. Or try Florida, they said. Find a nice place in Boca. Relax. Play mahjong. Watch the waves. Well, the only game I know how to play is poker. I'd spent my whole life dealing with crime waves, and now they were telling me to go sit in the sand and watch the ocean. Ha! Thanks but no thanks, I told them. And that's when I joined NAP. They have many younger agents, of course, but the people at NAP weren't afraid of someone with a little experience."

"You're a secret agent!" I shouted. A secret agent was at the very top of my list of what would make a perfect nanny, right behind professional baseball player.

"Yeah, right," muttered Ali, still acting like a Super Snot.

Nanny X sounded like she was telling the truth. I wanted her to be. Because if she was, maybe we really could help Stinky. And the park. And who knew what else?

"Shhhh. Now that you know, I'm a not-so-secret agent," said Nanny X. "Actually, I prefer the term *special* agent. But I'm a nanny, too, I promise you. I've had all of the requisite courses in child care, nutrition, and CPR. We find it easier to carry out our investigations while working as nannies. It's an excellent cover, especially around here. A lot of important people come through the capital area, and we need to keep an eye on some of them. You'd be surprised at how much espionage equipment we can squeeze into a little diaper bag. That way we're not so conspicuous."

"Conspicuous" means you stand out. "Inconspicuous" is when you don't. Both of those were reading connection words last month, but our nanny didn't seem like she knew how to be inconspicuous, even if she did work for an undercover organization. I could help her out with that part, though. My friend Ethan and I had been practicing being inconspicuous in case of a zombie invasion. The people zombies always go after first are the ones who stand out. Plus people who are slow.

"Is it dangerous for the kids?" I asked. What I meant was: *us*. I wasn't really scared or anything, as long as it was daylight, but it seemed like the sort of question you should ask when your nanny turns out to be a special agent.

"It can be," said Nanny X. "I won't lie to you. That's why we carefully screen our families to make sure the children involved have certain abilities. That means bravery in the face of danger, and it also means wits to help them escape danger should the situation arise. Of course we do our best to make sure that the situation doesn't arise; I daresay a good number of our families are never aware there's a member of NAP working in their household. But sometimes these things can't be helped."

"And Ali and me? We have these certain abilities?" I crossed my fingers.

"But of course," said Nanny X. "Even Eliza has talents, in her own way. I've been watching you for some time, and I think you have a great many abilities. Can you tell me what they are?"

"Baseball," I said, right off the bat. "Plus, I'm the only member of our family who can speak like Donald Duck."

"I'm sure there will be times when your athleticism will

come in handy," Nanny X agreed. "And many of our best agents can speak other languages. What else?"

Sometimes Ethan and I rewrote nursery rhymes to include words like "fart," but I wasn't sure that counted.

"Jake's honest," Ali said. I was glad to hear her saying something. I couldn't believe it was actually something *nice*. "He didn't freak out that time he got staples in his head. And I guess he's a pretty good listener."

"Bravo," Nanny X said. "And what about you, Ali? What are your talents?"

"Not that any of this is real," Ali said, "but I do have excellent powers of persuasion." It's true. Like, she can get me to collect all of the garbage when it's not even my turn.

"What else?" said Nanny X.

Ali shrugged and went back to being all glary again.

"Ali can tie knots," I said. "And she can untie them. Plus, she notices things. Like a scientist." If Ali was being nice, I could be nice, too.

"Bravo again," said Nanny X. "We need people who are observant. Observant people are good at spotting things that are out of the ordinary. They're good at spotting *clues*. For instance, what can you tell me about the rock that hit the mayor, Alison?"

Ali rolled her eyes, but I think at least a little part of her wanted to believe Nanny X was a real special agent. The old-days Ali would have believed it. "Humor me," said Nanny X.

"It was a rock," Ali said.

Nanny X sighed. "I suppose that's a start."

Ali closed her eyes, to think about it, I guess, but then she opened them kind of wide. "It was round," she said. "Rounder than most rocks you find around here. And bigger. And it didn't even come from where Stinky was standing. It came from someplace higher."

She was right. If Stinky had pitched that rock, it would have gone up toward the stage and then down again. But this one just went down.

"If the rock that hit the mayor wasn't the one Stinky was carrying, the real rock could still be here someplace," I said.

The stage was empty, but that didn't mean anything. Maybe the Green-Not-Mean lady had kicked it when it bounced off the mayor. I searched around in the grass. Then I crawled under the stage to look there. It was dark, but I could still see things, like some twigs and a cigarette butt and—

"I found something!" I shouted.

It was round and brown, like the rock that had conked the mayor on the head. But unlike a rock, it was also kind of hairy looking. Because it turned out that it wasn't a rock at all; it was a coconut.

7. Alison

Nanny X Is a Certifiable Crazy Person

Great. We had a nanny who was not only a certifiable crazy person, she actually believed she was a *special agent*. I'll bet that's not what my mother meant when she told me the new nanny was special. I guess having Nanny X believe she was a special agent was a little better than having her believe she was George Washington, but not by much. At least it was a good reason for her not acting like a proper nanny. Not that any of that made me feel better.

Just then, Jake scooted out from under the stage with a coconut. He was pushing it with a stick, like he was playing pool in caveman times. Looking at him, you might have thought he was being smart about not messing up any fingerprints— except I wasn't sure you could leave fingerprints on a coconut. Also, Jake had this thing for sticks. They reminded him of baseball bats, I guess. Nanny X pulled a plastic bag from inside her diaper bag and eased the coconut into it.

"Evidence," she said. "Are there any others?"

Okay, so she found her "something out of the ordinary." That didn't mean that she really worked for NAP. It didn't mean anything at all, except that we needed a new nanny.

Jake crawled under the stage again and moved from end to end. "Nope. I don't see anything else," he said. When he crawled out, he was covered with dirt, and he had a leaf stuck in his curly hair. He looked at Yeti and pointed to the coconut.

"Find it, boy," he said. "Go find another coconut." *Oh, please.* Yeti started sniffing all around, even though he's a Samoyed, not a bloodhound. He sniffed up and down and around trees. Eliza, who was back in her stroller, started fussing, so Nanny X let her out again, and she toddled after Yeti yelling, "Arf, arf!" Yeti stopped near an extra-tall oak tree with branches that stretched toward us. He ran around and around, barking.

"Good try, Yeti," Jake said. "But I don't see anything."

Yeti put his paws on the side of the tree and whined.

I looked at Nanny X. It was obvious we weren't leaving the park until we found another "clue," so I decided to play along. Anything to get us out of there faster.

"Maybe we don't need to look *around* the tree," I said. "Maybe we need to look up *in* the tree."

"That's it!" Jake started climbing. Mom says he should've been a monkey. I started climbing, too. Why not, right? We were at a park. And climbing is good exercise.

But my brother was ahead of me. He shimmied out onto a branch and parted the green leaves above us. "Aha!" he said, which is not a word I've ever heard him use. But I guess it's an okay word if you're pretending to be a special agent and you've found another clue. A few minutes later I wanted to use it, too, because I spotted a coconut of my own. It was in a hollow of the tree, where a squirrel would have put it if he had an extra-big mouth and could actually carry a coconut. But a squirrel hadn't put it there. So who had?

Nanny X passed her evidence bags up to me, and I passed one on up to Jake. We slid the coconuts inside. Then we climbed down. At the bottom of the tree, we found something else: a brown, bruised banana peel.

"Whoever catapulted that coconut was hungry," Nanny X said.

From somewhere in the diaper bag, we heard the ringing of a telephone. Nanny X reached in and pulled out her folded diaper. Now that we were close, we could see tiny metal buttons on the diaper's liner, and small holes for sound. *A secret phone.* Okay, if this was make-believe, her props seemed pretty real. But she couldn't possibly—

"Hello?" she said into the diaper. "Yes. Of course they're with me. What kind of a nanny do you think I am?"

She paused, and I knew it was because this time the diaper really *was* talking back. You know that expression "her jaw dropped"? Mine really did.

"Coconuts," Nanny X was saying. "Three of them, just like on Roosevelt Island."

Pause.

"I was afraid of that. We'll use the utmost caution."

Pause.

"Is he at the hospital?"

Pause.

"He's a stubborn man. We'll meet him there. X out."

She closed the diaper, which I guess meant she hung up.

"It's just as I feared," she said. "Coconuts. We can't be certain, of course, but it looks like we're dealing with a very powerful crime syndicate."

With coconuts. Right.

"What's a syndicate?" asked Jake.

"In this case it's a big group of bad guys."

"Coconut-eating bad guys?"

"Coconut-*throwing* bad guys," said Nanny X. "At least that's what happened on Roosevelt Island. There was a counterfeiting operation there, and when we got too close, the coconuts started flying. I . . . we lost them."

I hadn't seen anything like that in the news.

"Do you think that's why the mayor got hit?" Jake asked. "Because he got too close to something?"

"Sure," I said. "A crazy gang of coconut counterfeiters is trying to knock him off."

Jake gave me a mean look, but he didn't speak.

"Right now it's about as clear as coconut milk," said Nanny X. "But I'm sure it will begin to make sense. Let's go see the mayor."

"Us, too?" I said.

"What?" Nanny X said. "You think I'm going to leave you on your own with a bunch of coconut hoodlums lurking around? Of course you're coming. Besides, you might notice something I don't. And you know Daniel Malloy. We should talk to him as well."

"Nanny . . . X?" I said as she reached into the diaper bag and handed Eliza a baby cracker. Jake and I were going to have to tap into Eliza's supply if we didn't get some more food soon.

"Hmm?" our nanny said.

"Why don't you just use your normal cell phone?"

"I do sometimes," she said. "But a regular cell phone can't do all of the things my diaper phone can do."

"What can it do?" I asked her.

"It can take pictures," she said.

"Cell phones take pictures."

"Infrared pictures," she said. "It also has a protected signal that cannot be intercepted, and a bypass option that lets it circumnavigate the switchboard at dozens of government agencies, including the White House. And it fits snugly around a baby's tush in case of emergencies. This one is just Eliza's size, you see?"

"But what happens if the baby—"

"Yes?"

"What if the baby *poops*?" Jake finished my sentence for me.

"Or pees," I agreed. "Wouldn't that damage your 'equipment'?"

"Heavens no," said Nanny X. "It's waterproof. And my phone can do one more thing a cell phone can't. If it gets into the wrong hands, that is."

"What does it do?" Jake and I asked together.

"It blows up," said Nanny X. "Now come, children, or we'll miss our chance to see the mayor."

8. Jake

Nanny X Takes on City Hall

I tried to forget that my little sister could be wearing a butt-bomb. She wiggled around just like normal, and lifted her arms up to be held when we parked the stroller at City Hall. Nanny X carried her right up to the mayor's office.

"Hello?" she called.

"Yes? Who's there?" the mayor answered from a room in the back.

We went in. "Nanny X," our nanny said. She pulled out a badge and flashed it. The mayor looked at it for a second while holding an ice pack up against his head. He started to hand the badge back, but Ali intercepted it. She held it to the light. Then she closed one eye and studied it. If she'd had a magnifying glass, I'll bet she would have used that, too.

"I want to see," I whispered, but she ignored me.

"So this is what NAP is doing with its time these days, is it?" asked Mayor Osbourne. I elbowed Ali in the ribs.

Now my S.S. sister would *have* to believe our nanny was a member of NAP. The mayor did. Ali elbowed me back.

"I'm sure I don't know what you mean," Nanny X said.

"There was an assassination attempt," the mayor said. "Involving a juvenile. But the culprit has been captured. We don't need the involvement of a secret organization."

"I beg to differ, Mr. Mayor," said Nanny X. "I believe the culprit, as you call him, is an innocent eleven-year-old boy. And, excuse me, 'assassination attempt'? I think we're dealing with something else here altogether."

"Such as?"

"We're still trying to find that out."

Ali rolled her eyes again, even though she'd seen the badge.

Just then the mayor's secretary came in. "Your smoothie, sir," she said, leaving it on his desk.

I loved smoothies. The empty space in my stomach, which had only been filled by one apple and exactly zero bites of peanut butter and anchovy sandwich, rumbled.

"Cheers." The mayor took the ice pack off his head, and we could see a purple goose egg where he'd been hit by the coconut. He gulped some smoothie through an extra-large straw, making a slurping sound even though the cup wasn't empty.

"That hits the spot," he said.

Yeti licked his lips. I licked mine. Eliza made a sound sort of like Yeti makes when he's locked in the bedroom, so Nanny X pulled a bottle out of the diaper bag and handed it to her.

"I'm sorry, children," the mayor said, gulping and slurping. "I'd offer to share, but . . . germs."

"Is it chocolate?" I asked.

"Ha," he said. "No, this was just delivered to me by the company that wants to set up a new business here in

Lovett. The very subject of the park meeting, in fact. I know I shouldn't show any favoritism by drinking it, but it seems a small compensation for the injuries I sustained. And it's just so darned good."

"Strawberry?" asked Ali. She looked at him the way she looks at me when she knows I've been in her room.

"Nope," said the mayor. "Actually, it's coconut."

"*Coconut!*" I said.

"Coconut," Ali whispered, and I could tell that she was finally starting to believe.

The mayor's eyes got sort of darkish. "Is there something *wrong* with coconut?"

"No but we—" I began, but Nanny X looked at me and I stopped.

"We just all like coconut, I guess," Ali said. "The coconut kids, that's what they call us. And, um, the coconut nanny."

"Not many children have a taste for coconut," said the mayor.

"Ah, but these children are extraordinary," Nanny X said.

"Then I'll let you in on a secret," said the mayor. "The company I'm talking about wants to set up a coconut processing and distribution center, right here, if we can get the zoning for it. Think about it: Lovett, Virginia, could be the coconut hub of the entire eastern seaboard. We could have a new slogan: The Coconut Capital!"

"Lovett already has a slogan," I said. Our slogan is You'll Love It in Lovett. It's on lots of bumper stickers.

"We could have coconut stands on every corner," said the mayor. "We could build a coconut monument and add ourselves to the D.C. monument tour. Think of the tourism! We could serve coconut ice cream. That'll get the kids liking coconut! We could host a Coconut Ball! On Easter we could send hundreds of coconuts to the president. They could roll coconuts instead of eggs on the White House lawn!" He took another sip of his smoothie, then rubbed his hands together.

And we'd thought our nanny was crazy. The mayor was nuts. *Coconuts.*

"What's the name of this coconut distributor?" Nanny X asked, kind of casually. But I knew the answer was important.

"Big Adam's Distribution," he said. "This smoothie came from Big Adam himself."

"And you get along with this Big Adam?" asked Nanny X. "He wouldn't try to harm you?"

"Harm? Say, what is this? Of course we get along."

"Just making sure," said Nanny X. "I know that you believe the, er, attempt on your life came from that young boy, but I have other suspicions. I just want to make sure you've checked out Big Adam thoroughly, that you're sure he's a legitimate business operator."

"Of course I'm sure," the mayor blustered, which is another reading connection word. "He gave me a full Power-Point presentation. A *PowerPoint.*"

"I see," Nanny X said. "Is there anything else you can tell us that will help our investigation? Anything at all?"

"Sure," the mayor said. He was really angry now. "Why don't you go investigate why birds fly south in the winter? Or why Nolan's Market was out of bananas this morning? Why don't you investigate that? Big Adam's Distribution is a legitimate company, and my guess is they'll be breaking ground for a new headquarters in that park by the beginning of May."

"Not if I have anything to do with it." Nanny X was angry, too. She moved out of the room so fast that the flowers on her hat looked like they were blowing in the wind.

9. Alison

Nanny X Smells Something Rotten

Okay, so maybe our nanny wasn't *totally* crazy. I guess she could have bought the badge on the Internet, but the mayor getting hit by a coconut one minute and drinking a coconut smoothie the next had to be more than a coincidence. If Nanny X thought the coconut was a real clue, well, maybe it was. Two things I didn't get, though: 1. If the mayor was friends with the coconut people, why would they want to knock him out? 2. If Nanny X was undercover, why did she show the mayor her badge?

Nanny X had spent the entire morning moving in slow motion. Now she was walking down the street so fast, Jake and I had to run to keep up with her. So did Yeti. Eliza rode along in the stroller, laughing all the way.

"Where are we going?" I asked.

"To talk to Daniel."

"Are you mad at the mayor?" asked Jake.

"He is arrogant and naïve," she said, puffing a little. "But he's right about one thing: We haven't proven anything about anything. I suppose I'm a bit mad at myself, going in with only half an accusation. But I'm certain Big Adam's Distribution is bad news."

"The initials even spell BAD," said Jake, who, like I said, is obsessed with initials.

Nanny X stopped so fast we nearly ran into her. "I hadn't thought of that." She parked the stroller by a low concrete wall, and pulled a flat packet of baby wipes out of the diaper bag. She opened the blue lid, but instead of wipes we saw a tiny keyboard and a computer screen.

"This gives me direct access to 149 crime databases all over the world," she said, punching in a code followed by the words "Big Adam's Distribution."

A moment later two dozen reports popped onto the screen. She opened a few of them, but they weren't complete. One labeled Profile just read:

> **Owner first name:** Big
> **Owner last name:** Adam
> **Manufacturing history:** Unknown
> **Full-time employees:** Unknown
> **Sector:** Industrial goods (and unknown)
> **Environmental impact:** Unknown
> **Summary:** Big Adam's Distribution filed corporation
> papers last year in 17 states, including Alaska,
> and looked, for a time, like a company to watch.
> However, the papers filed were incomplete, and
> though it was reported Mr. Adam had paid visits
> to industrial sites in both West Virginia and
> Wyoming, no known businesses opened as a result.
> Likewise, no state administrators recalled meeting
> Big Adam himself. Our crime investigation unit
> linked a company called B.A.D. with the so-called

"coconut bombings" on Roosevelt Island and an unparalleled theft from the Gudula Diamond Center in Italy, as well as the disappearance of famed geologist Hubert Snavely. But our unit has no proof at this point, only speculation that there is something nefarious at the root of Mr. Adam's company. Mr. Adam himself has been hard to trace, and is rarely spotted in public.

Code: Old mackerel

"Is that for real?" I said. Just when I was starting to believe her, she brings up a website that talks about fish.

"This particular database ranks suspects by odor instead of by color or number," Nanny X explained. "Old mackerel has one of the foulest odors imaginable. The fact that they used mackerel as opposed to, say, some type of cheese tells me plenty. The use of a fish indicates that there's something fishy about Big Adam, which, of course, we already know. And as you can see, they suspect plenty but they've proven nothing. It'll be up to us to do that."

I wondered why someone who knew all about fish odor packed anchovies for lunch, but I didn't ask. Nanny X flipped down the top of the baby wipes and marched us into the police station. Stinky's mother was standing in front of the desk, talking to one of the officers. She had the same dark eyes as Stinky, and the same smile, only now she wasn't using it; she was yelling. Stinky's nanny, Boris, stood next to her, talking calmly. With his island accent he always sounded calm, even when he wasn't.

"Oh, but he's never been in trouble of any sort," Boris was saying. "He has no previous offenses, you have no right to hold him—"

"Tell it to the judge," the officer said.

"You bet we will," said Mrs. Malloy. "Where is she?" The officer pointed, and Mrs. Malloy walked out of the office. Boris followed, giving a slight nod to Nanny X and a wink to me and Jake. I waved, wondering why Boris hadn't been with Stinky when the whole thing started.

Nanny X approached the officer slowly. The flowers on her gardening hat gave her some extra height.

"We're here to see Daniel Malloy," she said.

"You have to be authorized to do that," said the officer, whose mustache covered half his face. "Or you have to be his mother. And you're not. The mother went that way." He pointed in the direction Mrs. Malloy had gone. "So if I had to make a guess, I'd guess you're authorized to leave."

"Oh, I'm authorized to do much more than leave." Nanny X reached into her diaper bag and yanked out the badge she had shown to the mayor. It flashed in the fluorescent light.

"Oh, I'm so *sorry*, ma'am." Now the policeman sounded overly polite, like he was trying to be nice, but it was pretty obvious he didn't want to be. "I didn't realize you were with *NAP*."

"There are probably a great many things you don't realize," Nanny X said.

"And these children?" the officer asked, glaring at us.

"These children are with me. Any courtesy extended to NAP officials must also be extended to them."

"And I suppose the dog—"

"The dog, too."

I didn't think we were going to get in, but the officer stood up and led us down the hall, mumbling things like "no choice" and "government" and "they could have at least sent the FBI or the CIA."

We found Stinky Malloy in a tiny room inside the police station. They hadn't put him in a jail cell. But the room didn't have any windows, and it smelled like a school cafeteria before all of the garbage is thrown away. There was a chair in there, the hard plastic kind. Stinky sat on the floor with his arms around his knees.

"Hi," I said.

"Hi." For some reason he looked smaller than normal, maybe because he wasn't towering over me the way he usually did. His hair was in his eyes and his chin stuck out a little, like he was ready for a fight. "I'm glad you were able to make it to the meeting."

"This is our nanny," I told him.

"Hello, Daniel," our nanny said. "You may call me Nanny X."

Stinky stood up and shook her hand. "Did you see Boris?" he asked. "And my mom? They were just here."

"And now they're with the judge," said Nanny X. "But I expect they'll be back soon. Meanwhile, we'd like to ask you a few questions, if we may."

"Go ahead. Everyone else has."

"How did you know the park was in trouble?" she asked.

"I'm very concerned about the environment," he said. "And it wasn't a secret, was it? It was in the newspaper."

"Ah," said Nanny X. "Go on."

"We live right behind that park. If they put a factory there, we'll be living behind a factory."

"So you would stand to lose a lot if the park became a factory?"

"Sure I would," Stinky said. "So would the whole town."

"Touché," Nanny X said. "But that does speak to motive. Now: You didn't throw any rocks at the mayor?" The way she asked it, it didn't sound like a real question. Stinky seemed to know she was on his side.

"I only picked up one rock today," he said. "I was still holding it when they grabbed me."

"And they assumed—"

"They thought since I was holding that rock, I must have thrown the first one. But that's not why I had it."

"You thought it was a geode?" Nanny X remembered. Of course she did—she remembered everything.

"Exactly," Stinky said. "I was saving it for later. Sometimes you can't tell it's really a geode until you crack it open. Now they're saying I can't even have it back. It's evidence."

Then *I* remembered something. "What hand were you holding the sign with?" I asked him.

"My right," he said. "I'm a righty."

"And you had the geode in your left hand?"

"Yeah," he said. "It was too big to fit in my pocket." He looked down at his jeans. "I guess these are kind of small," he said.

"Then you couldn't have thrown the rock," said Jake. "It's hard to pitch when your hands are full."

"Exactly," I said. Sometimes my brother and I still think alike. Unfortunately, all of this mentioning of hands made me want to chew my fingernails, but I fought it and kept talking. "You couldn't have thrown anything at the mayor, even if you wanted to."

"Well, *maybe* he could have," Jake said, backtracking and spoiling the whole idea. "But he couldn't have thrown it very *hard*," he added, unspoiling it. "Whoever hit the mayor had a really hard throw; otherwise he wouldn't have gotten knocked out."

Out of the corner of my eye, I could see Nanny X smiling again. "Make sure you pass that nugget on to your lawyer, Daniel," she said. Then her lips resumed their normal position. "You do agree someone threw something, though, correct?"

"Sure, anyone could see that," Stinky said. "I don't think it was a rock, though."

Jake and I exchanged looks. Yeti drooled on Eliza's foot.

"Why not?"

"Well," said Stinky, "if it was a rock and it was really as big as it looked, the person who threw it would have to be really strong or use an industrial-strength slingshot or something. Most of the people at that protest didn't look like they could throw very well. No offense."

"We don't think the mayor was hit by a rock, either!" I blurted out.

"See!" Stinky said. He pushed his hair out of his eyes. "What do you think it was?"

Jake and I looked at Nanny X to see if it was okay to tell. She gave us the nanny nod. "A coconut," we said.

"Hmm," Stinky said. "Coconuts are heavy, but they're not as dense as rocks, even with the milk still inside them." He paused a minute. "But why would someone throw a coconut at the mayor?"

I shrugged. That was what we were trying to figure out.

"Did you happen to see what direction it came from?" Nanny X asked.

"No," Stinky said. "I was looking toward the stage, not away from it. And my sign was kind of blocking my vision."

"Could it have come out of a tree?" asked Nanny X.

"Maybe. Why not? You're going to explain all of this to the mayor, aren't you? Maybe he'll believe an adult."

"He believes what he believes," Nanny X said. "But don't worry. When we get all of our facts, he'll have to see it our way. And when he does, he'll stop this ridiculous nonsense and drop the charges."

"I hope it's soon," Stinky said. "The planning commission is supposed to make its decision tonight, and I want to be there with my sign." He let out a breath, like he'd been holding it all afternoon. "It's a lucky thing you guys were at the park."

"It's a lucky thing Nanny X was there, too," Jake said. I didn't want to admit it, but I was starting to agree with him.

10. Jake

Nanny X Goes Bananas

Nanny X thought we should go to Nolan's Market. That seemed like an okay idea because we'd found that banana peel in the park, plus, we needed more secret-agent supplies. Like food. I had a jar of plain, un-anchovied peanut butter under my bed from when Ethan and I were getting prepared for the zombie invasion. If we had a chance to go home I could get it, but we weren't going home.

Ali and I did odds and evens to see who got to go into the grocery store and who had to stay outside with Yeti. I picked odds, so I was the one who got hit by the fried-chicken smell when the automatic doors opened up. But Nanny X didn't care about the fried chicken. She went straight to the manager, who was in a little glass office where she could watch over the whole store. "I want to talk to you about your banana situation," Nanny X said.

"Yes, we have no bananas," the manager said, which sounded like the song. She had a name tag that said

Rosalita. "The truck comes tomorrow. You will have to wait until then."

"Yes, but *why* do you have no bananas?" asked Nanny X. "Is there a shortage?"

"No shortage," said Rosalita. "Big customer. He came in this morning and bought every banana in the whole place."

"Can you tell me his name?" Nanny X asked. "Or what he was planning on doing with all of those bananas?"

"I cannot," Rosalita said. "To tell you would not be respecting the privacy of my customers."

"Did he say *why* he wanted the bananas?" I asked. Sometimes you have to ask the same question different ways to get an answer. I learned that from my mom, who did it in the lawyer business, and from my Super Snot sister, who didn't usually answer me the first time I asked her something.

"Well, they are *very good* bananas," Rosalita said. "But all he said to me was that he had a hungry crew. I will tell you this one other thing: He said it was a *small* crew. And yet he bought 864 bananas."

"Eight hundred—" Nanny X said.

"Eight hundred sixty-four."

Who would eat 864 bananas? I thought. And then I answered: *I would.* Because right then I was feeling like I could eat 864 bananas all by myself. "Nanny X," I said, "as long as we're here, could we please get some food? Ali and I are kind of starving."

She raised that same eyebrow and looked at me. "You didn't eat your sandwich," she said.

"No," I said. "It was . . . no."

"You'll grow to love it," Nanny X said. "But for now, go wait outside with Alison. Eliza and I will round up another snack."

"Ahm!" Eliza shook her head so that her red curls bounced all around.

I'm counting on you, kid, I thought to Eliza. *Bring us back something good.*

I was hoping for Pringles, which we eat a lot of because of our last name, or even just some granola. I tried not to blame Eliza when Nanny X walked out of the store with a bag of radishes and a tin of sardines. What was it with this nanny and canned fish?

"Great," said Ali, who was not blaming Eliza but who seemed to be blaming *me*. Again. "This is just what we *always* eat for a snack after school."

"What do you mean?" said Nanny X. Being a special agent, she seemed to know all about sarcasm. "This is brain food."

I wasn't sure how food was going to help my brain if it never even made it into my stomach, but I couldn't say that. So I said: "You can smell sardines from pretty far away. Maybe they're not the best spy food."

"I have mints," our nanny said. "But you're right, Jake Z. We'd better stick to radishes in case we need to be inconspicuous."

"Great," Ali said, glaring at me again. "Radishes."

At first I tried to pretend the radishes were marshmallows or a plate of nachos or something. But they tasted like dirt. Really bitter dirt. By the time we'd climbed the steps to Mr. Strathmore's office, I'd stopped pretending the radishes were anything but what they were: a gross, awful garden snack. I could probably find a better way to describe them, but I couldn't find a better acronym: GAGS.

11. Alison

Nanny X Eavesdrops

Apparently Nanny X has the shopping skills of a rabbit, or maybe a harbor seal, because no human being would want the food she bought. Still, I followed her to Mr. Strathmore's office at the Chamber of Commerce, which was a tall, thin, brick building squashed between Colliton's Bike Shop and Robinson Funeral Home.

Since he'd been onstage looking at the crowd (until he started fighting with the anti-factory lady and the mayor got hit), Nanny X thought Mr. Strathmore might have seen something. It was pretty clear to me the only thing he saw was dollar signs.

He was sitting in his office, still dressed in his suit. But he wasn't alone. A man was in there with him.

The man wore a Hawaiian shirt, and he smelled like he'd taken a bath in suntan lotion. His eyes were small and beady, like Jason Geddy's hamster's.

He was short but he had big hands, and one of those

hands was holding a tall glass of something. You didn't have to be a special agent to figure out that it was a coconut smoothie.

"Good afternoon," said Nanny X, not flashing her badge for once. "We are concerned citizens who were at the rally this afternoon."

"I'm sorry, miss, this is a private meeting," said Mr. Strathmore, who was also drinking a smoothie.

"So polite," Nanny X said to us. "You see, children? Good manners are important when you deal with the public." She turned back to Mr. Strathmore. "Excuse me, but we won't take up much of your time. We hoped you could tell us some more about that interesting company that wants to set up shop here." She turned to the Hawaiian-shirt man. "Or perhaps you could tell us?"

The man grinned at Nanny X, showing off a mouthful of perfect teeth. "Who, me?" he said. "It could be that I'm just a concerned citizen like yourself, trying to make sure that Lovett is open for business. It's business that rules the world, you know."

"Business that drives the economy," agreed Mr. Strathmore.

"Business that gives you power," said the stranger. "Business that is king!" He laughed. "We're sure you'll see it our way, once we replace the park with a factory and a small airstrip. All kids love airplanes."

"But there are two airports nearby already," Nanny X said. "And the noise—"

"—will be the noise of progress!" said Mr. Strathmore. "Now, I'm sorry, but you really must go. Like I said, this meeting is private. You'll have to make an appointment." He shut the door, but we could still hear them talking. Part of it sounded like "blah, blah, blah," but we distinctly heard the words "Listen, Big Adam."

The man in the Hawaiian shirt was Big Adam. Something told me that Nanny X knew all along.

"You don't have any drinking glasses in that diaper bag, do you?" I asked her.

"Are you thirsty?"

I was, but that wasn't the point. "For listening. I've tried it; it really works." I didn't mention that I'd tried it on my parents when I was trying to find out more about our nanny situation. I didn't overhear anything, except that my mother was not hiring a woman named Lola because she refused to change diapers.

"I don't approve of eavesdropping," Nanny X said, "unless we're doing it for professional purposes. Which we are." She fished around in the diaper bag for a minute and came out with a purple sippy cup with a juggling panda on the front. "Voilà."

From the outside, it looked like an ordinary sippy cup. But inside, there was a jumble of wires. She reached into the cup part and pulled out a teething cracker, which she slid under the door.

"Follow me," she said. "Quickly."

We followed her down the hall and stopped outside the bathroom.

"I can't go into the ladies' room," Jake announced.

"Fine," said Nanny X. She led all of us into the men's room.

"But *you* can't come in *here*," Jake said.

"This is an extraordinary situation, Jake Z. Desperate times. Desperate measures." For once, I agreed with Nanny X. I hadn't been inside of a men's room since I was about Eliza's age. One thing I noticed right away was that they had pink soap, just like they have in the ladies' room.

After the bathroom door swung shut, Nanny X fitted the top part of the sippy cup into the bottom part—only upside down, so it looked like a tiny satellite dish. At first all we heard was static. But Nanny X pushed a button on the panda's nose, and the top part of the cup started rotating. Two voices came through the speaker, clear as day.

"The mayor's completely sold on my plan."

"So am I, Big Adam."

I knew those beady eyes meant something bad, the B.A.D. kind of bad.

"You may call me Coconut King if you'd rather. Or King for short. How many votes have we got?"

"We've got three of the five committee members. Kathleen Walker is undecided. And Hans Baxter is against. But I haven't been able to reach Hans today—he appears to be missing."

"Is that so?" said Big Adam with an evil laugh. "It's locked up, then. In five hours, the path will be cleared and my empire will have found a new home."

"Cheers," said Mr. Strathmore.

"Cheers," said Big Adam.

"Eeee eeee." The sound that came over the speaker was almost human, but it could have been a squeaky desk chair. Yeti's ears perked up and he turned his head sideways, but he didn't bark.

"Hush," said Big Adam. "Now. That woman who was just here—I didn't like her. She was too nosy."

I looked at Nanny X over the sippy cup, and she put her finger to her lips.

"She might cause trouble," Big Adam continued. "We need to make sure she stays out of the way."

"What trouble could she cause?" said Mr. Strathmore. "She's a grandmother or a baby-sitter or something."

"Yes, but I saw those children she was with talking to that other kid," said Big Adam. "The one who . . . took out the mayor. They may have been in on it."

"I don't see how that's possible," said Mr. Strathmore. "And while we're at it, I don't think that kid was responsible, either. Something about it just doesn't add up."

"You don't think the kid was responsible?"

"No," said Mr. Strathmore. "I really don't. I was on that stage when the mayor got hit. The angle was all wrong for the kid to have done it. And why would he have bothered? It doesn't make sense. Listen, Big Adam—"

"King."

"Listen, King. Goodness knows Lovett wants your business, and you know we want to accommodate you in any way we can, but I can't see doing it at the expense of Lovett's children. We're already taking their park. We can't be throwing kids in jail and getting grandmothers out of the way, can we? That's not what a friendly community does."

"I'm telling you, we need to keep our enemies where we can see them. That's good business."

"The missing commission member—Hans Baxter—you wouldn't know anything about his whereabouts, would you?"

"Don't ask questions you don't want answered."

"Then you—"

"I'll tell you what, Strat," Big Adam interrupted. "I'm going to make a little pit stop, and when I come back, I'm hoping you'll stop asking questions and see things my way. My little friend will stay here to keep you company."

What little friend was he talking about? We hadn't seen anyone else in the office.

"Are you threatening me?" Mr. Strathmore asked.

"So what if I am?"

"If you are, I'm not sure how much I want you for a business partner after all."

"You back out now," said Big Adam, "and you'll see what I can do with a coconut."

12. Jake

Nanny X Hides Out

The men's room had a really long row of urinals, plus one private stall with a door on it. When Big Adam said he had to make a pit stop, Nanny X pulled us all in there, even Yeti, and latched the door. You know that scene in *From the Mixed-Up Files of Mrs. Basil E. Frankweiler* where Claudia and Jamie are hiding in the museum and they have to stand on the toilet seat so the guards won't see their feet? We had to do that, except our toilet couldn't hold one nanny plus three kids plus one big, slobbery dog.

"I'll stay down here," I said. Ali's sneakers had a pink stripe on them, Eliza had baby feet, and Nanny X's feet looked like they belonged in that museum with Claudia and Jamie. At least my feet looked like boy feet.

Nanny X climbed onto the toilet seat first, holding Eliza, and Ali climbed up after them. We hoped Eliza wouldn't make any noise. We hoped Yeti wouldn't, either.

The "eeee eeee" noise came through the sippy cup

again. Then there was a clunk as Nanny X grabbed the cup and fitted it together the proper way, sealing it in silence. She crammed it into the diaper bag, and a noise came from inside there that sounded like she'd stepped on something alive. Then that sound faded, too.

"Act natural," Nanny X told me. "You're doing fine."

The door to the men's room opened, and we heard footsteps. The footsteps stopped somewhere near the urinals, but we didn't hear anyone doing the sort of thing people usually do when they're in front of urinals. Instead, we heard a weird clacking and rattling sound.

Ali put one foot on each side of the stall, and then one hand on each side, the way she does in the door frame at home. She shimmied higher, her hands and feet like suction cups, so she could see just over the top and out into the bathroom.

I wanted to know what she was seeing, but I couldn't ask her; Big Adam would have heard. Then Eliza squirmed. Nanny X moved just a bit to get a better hold on her, and Ali lost her grip on the wall at the very same time. When she shimmies back home in the door frame, she is usually barefoot. Maybe the rubber on her sneakers wasn't as suction-y as her feet. She landed on top of Yeti, who yelped.

"Who's there?" Big Adam's footsteps came closer and closer. They stopped right outside our bathroom stall.

"*Take me out to the ball game,*" I sang, instead of answering. Sometimes singing makes me less nervous.

He pounded on the door of the stall.

"*Take me out with the crowd.*" I sang louder, the way I sing when we go hiking and everyone is counting on me to scare away the bears. "*Buy me some peanuts and—*"

"Step out here," said Big Adam.

I looked at Ali, who just stared at the bathroom floor

like a statue, and then at Nanny X. "It's OK," the nanny whispered. "We've got your back."

I flushed the toilet, because that seemed like a good cover and also a way to cover up noise in case Eliza was thinking about making some. Then I unlocked the stall door and pushed it open just a little. I slid through to face Big Adam.

"You were making a pretty good racket in there," Big Adam said.

I held my breath. I'm pretty sure Nanny X held her breath, too. Then Yeti squeezed out under the bottom of the stall. Maybe he didn't like being in such a small space. Or maybe he didn't want me to be alone, which is more than I can say for a certain older sister.

"Arf!"

Yeti's paws clacked on the tile. With no one holding his leash, he ran all around the bathroom. He was making so much noise, Big Adam couldn't have heard Eliza if she was having her five o'clock meltdown.

"I can't believe Stratty let you into his office with that dog. And now you have a dog in a public bathroom."

"I'm sorry," I said.

"It's unsanitary," he said. He slapped his ankle, like someone slapping a mosquito. "Fleas," Big Adam said. "That's one reason dogs aren't allowed in here."

"But Yeti doesn't have any—"

"You take that dog and come along."

"But I'm not finished," I said, even though I'd flushed.

"Yes," he said. "I believe you are." He looked at me again, closer. "What did you see?"

"The toilet?" I said. Maybe Ali had seen something when she was being the lookout, but I hadn't.

"Where's that woman you were with? Your grandmother?"

"My nanny," I said. "And she's waiting for me."

"I think we should take a little walk, don't you?" Big Adam said.

"I'm not supposed to go anyplace with strangers," I said. But Big Adam grabbed me by the arm and led me out of the bathroom. In my brain I thought: *Bravery in the face of danger.* Then I thought it two more times. I wanted to yell for Nanny X, but I didn't. I wanted to yell "H.M.A.," which stands for Help Me, Ali. Since she was being less of a Super Snot, I thought she would. But my sister didn't come after me. Yeti did, though. I grabbed his leash right up. "It's okay, boy," I told him. It wasn't. My sister was ignoring me, and Nanny X didn't have my back *or* my front. Only one person had me, and that person was Big Adam.

13. Alison

Nanny X Has a Plan

"How could you let them go?" My voice echoed in the bathroom. We'd started with a nanny who couldn't make a decent lunch. We'd ended up with a special agent who couldn't protect my little brother.

"Yeti is with him," Nanny X said calmly. "Don't worry; they haven't left the building yet."

I glared at her. "Why didn't you do anything? There were four of us. We could have taken him."

"He could have taken *you*."

"At least we would have been together," I said. "You should have stopped him."

"I still can. Do you trust me?"

"Why should I?" I asked. Her gray eyes stared into mine. I'm not sure what I saw in there, exactly, but something made me say: "Yes."

"Good. We have to find out what Big Adam is up to. I'm not going to leave Jake alone. Or you." She pulled out her diaper phone and pushed a blue button, which, I hoped, was not the button that would make it explode.

She handed me Eliza.

"I've just arranged for one of my co-operatives to meet you here. There's a homing device on Yeti's collar. If you have to, you'll be able to keep track of him with this." She pulled a bib out of the diaper bag and handed it to me. On the front, I saw a dribble of strained spinach and what looked like strained carrot. Then I noticed that the spinach stain was moving. So was a third stain next to it, which looked a little like squash. I guessed another thing our nanny couldn't do was laundry.

"That's Yeti with Jake," Nanny X said, pointing to the spinach. "You'll be able to see a map of Lovett if you hold this under a purple light. There's one in the bag."

"Who's that?" I asked, pointing to the squash stain, which, like the spinach stain, had stopped moving.

"Big Adam," she said.

"How are you tracking him?"

"Ah," she said. "I used what we like to call the Flick-a-Flea. The gold diaper pin has a secret compartment, you see. You just aim, press, and *ptuey*! A flea-sized tracking device. Right above his ankle. And this," she added, pointing to the carrot stain, "is me. There's a tracking device in my hat."

"But why would I need a tracking device for you?" I asked her. "You're right here."

Nanny X put on her sunglasses again. I looked at the bib. The stains were on the move. "I have to hurry before they leave the building," she said. "Stay out of sight until I'm gone. The operative will meet you right here in a few minutes. You're perfectly safe. There's a chance I can shake Jake free, but if I can't—"

"Nanny X . . ." The part of me that wasn't mad at her wanted to apologize, to tell her that it had really been my fault Jake had been taken away, because I'd made so much noise. But the words didn't come. I hadn't wanted a nanny. But that didn't mean I wanted to lose her, either.

"You're not losing me, Ali," Nanny X said, reading my mind again. "It's a plan. It's all part of the plan."

"Then how come you didn't mention the plan before?" I said.

"Because I just thought of it." She put a hand on Eliza's head. Then she handed me the whole diaper bag. I put it on my shoulder. Then she and her gardening hat and her motorcycle jacket moved quickly down the hallway. When I looked at the bib, the carrot stain seemed to be dripping down the front, chasing after the spinach and the squash.

14. Jake

Nanny X Gets Taken for a Ride

Some people run when they get scared, but that's kind of hard to do when a coconut freak has a super-villain death grip on your shoulder. Other people throw up or get strength they never knew they had. I wished for that last one, which would also come in handy in case of a zombie invasion, but I didn't get it. Some people start seeing things, and that's what I got. Big Adam led me out of the bathroom and down the hall. We were almost to Mr. Strathmore's office when I spotted this tiny, hairy guy. He was shorter than Big Adam, and he was totally, completely, absolutely naked. Mr. Strathmore was next to him, lying on the ground. He was either taking a nap right there on the floor, or else someone (the tiny naked hairy guy?) had knocked him out.

When we reached them, Big Adam stopped. "Well done," he said, which was strange, because people don't usually talk to other people's imagination.

"Woooooooowwww!" said Tiny Naked Hairy Guy. I

blinked. He was not a guy at all; he was a monkey. Or wait: a chimp, actually. The difference is that monkeys have tails. You don't live as close to the National Zoo as I do without having some of it rub off. Plus, he wasn't completely naked; he had a red bandana tied around his neck.

"Eeeee eeee eeee." The chimp pulled back his lips and looked at me. In one hand he held a coconut. He lifted his other hand and waved at me. I waved back.

"Arf! Arf!" Yeti barked at my imagination. His bark turned into a growl when the chimp walked up to us and tried to touch Yeti's back.

"No," said Big Adam, sounding all Darth Vader and stuff. "Leave them to me." The chimp took back his hand.

Big Adam pointed to Mr. Strathmore. "Get him out of here." He made some sort of hand gesture—sort of like the letter Q in sign language. The chimp dropped the coconut and dragged Mr. Strathmore toward what must have been the back of the building. Chimps are twice as strong as humans, according to my Fantastically Freaky book.

"Hurry *up*, you banana-eating hair ball," said Big Adam.

I felt sorry for the chimp; he had a lousy boss. While the chimp was dragging Mr. S down the hall, I tried to send my brain waves to my sisters, in case they were listening, and to Nanny X.

Back door, I thought. *Back door.*

I didn't feel like singing the ball game song anymore, but sometimes whistling calms me down, too, even if I can't make the actual whistling sound. *Phh. Phh. Phhhhhh.* I added it to the list of skills I needed but didn't have.

"I can just wait for my nanny right here," I said.

"I don't think so," Big Adam said. "Now you've *definitely* seen too much. Come on."

Phh. Phhh. Phhhhhh.

I hoped Ali would enjoy her life without a pesky little brother. Now she could take down her Keep Out sign until Eliza learned to read.

We reached the exit ahead of the chimp. Big Adam tightened his grip on my arm and then shoved the door open with his shoulder. Even though it hadn't been dark in the Chamber of Commerce building, the sun was so bright it felt like I was walking out of a movie. A bad movie. I shut my eyes and opened them again. There stood Nanny X. The flowers on her hat looked like they had grown. The sun reflected off her mirrored glasses. She stood with her legs apart and her arms folded, in front of a brown van the color of a . . . well, sure. The color of a coconut. I don't know how she got there ahead of us, but I was saved!

"Let the boy go," she said.

"I don't think that would be wise," Big Adam said. "Not yet. You know what they say: a *Cocos nucifera* in hand."

"Bird in hand," said Nanny X.

"Whatever."

The chimp galumphed out of the building, still lugging Mr. Strathmore.

"Well, that certainly explains the banana shortage, doesn't it, Jake Z?" said Nanny X. She turned back to Big Adam. "Let the boy go. It's my first day on the job, and I'm going to get fired if you kidnap him. Take me instead."

"Why don't I just take you both?" he said. He pulled out what looked like a tiny coconut with a long fuse on the end. "At least until after the board votes."

I wasn't saved. But at least I had some company.

The chimp let go of Mr. Strathmore and started pulling Nanny X toward the van. Nanny X did not resist. I was still holding Yeti by the leash. Big Adam looked at him, and I could almost hear him thinking *unsanitary flea bag*. But I guess he'd seen enough movies where the dog sounds the alarm and leads the police to the boy. In the end, he shoved us all into the van.

The chimp dragged Mr. Strathmore in next to us.

"Keep an eye on 'em," said Big Adam as he got into the driver's seat. "And remember"—he patted the seat next to him, and I saw a mound of coconuts piled up like cannonballs at those historic sites my parents take us to sometimes—"I'm armed."

I gave Nanny X a look that said *Let's tackle that chimp!*

She shook her head. As Big Adam gunned the motor, she leaned over and whispered: "Don't worry, Jake. This is our chance to find out what Big Adam is up to."

"But what about Eliza and—"

"No talking," Big Adam said.

The only good part of the ride was that Big Adam finally offered me one of his famous smoothies. The bad part was that we lurched around so many curves, I kind of wished he hadn't.

15. Alison

Nanny X Is Missing

The part of me that isn't good at taking orders wanted to run out of the bathroom and chase after Nanny X. But it was tricky since I was supposed to be taking care of my little sister. Besides, Nanny X had left the building. The spinach stain, the squash stain, and the carrot stain were racing across the bib now. Purple light = map of Lovett. Right.

Eliza and I sat down on the tile floor of the men's room and started sifting through the diaper bag. Teddy bear? No light and probably dangerous. Baby powder? Dangerous. Diapers? Lethal. Baby food? Disgusting.

I opened a book called *Moo, Sweet Cow*, and—

MOOOOOOOOOOOOOOOOOOOOOO. It was the sort of sound a cow would make if it was about the size of Godzilla. Not "sweet"; scary. The walls of the bathroom shook. Eliza started to cry. I slammed the book shut, but no one came running in to catch us or help us. The building must have been deserted. Finally I found a bunch of pacifiers. The yellow ones were labeled Stinky Binky. But there was one purple pacifier marked Blazing Binky. That looked promising. Gently, I squeezed the sucky part. A soft purple light began to glow. I held it over the bib and found the stains, which were now moving across a map of Lovett. Somehow they'd gotten all the way over to Turner Street. We couldn't catch them on foot.

I went back to the bag and got more of the crackers that Nanny X had allowed Eliza to eat earlier. We each ate one, after I took a tiny bite to make sure it wasn't another listening device. Which made me think about the first one.

Nanny X had said "Wait here," but "here" didn't necessarily mean the bathroom, did it? "Here" could have just meant the building in general. And our teething biscuit was still sitting on the floor of Mr. Strathmore's office. If Eliza and I got it back, we'd be doing something. And maybe we could use it again.

The hall was quiet. Mr. Strathmore's door was open but the light was off. Still, the light from the hallway lit it up enough that I could see the teething biscuit. Someone had stomped on it. There were crumbs and, if you looked closely, wires. Even if I hadn't seen the wires, I would have known it was a fake: Nothing can destroy a real teething biscuit. I didn't need an eavesdropping device to hear the sound that came next, though: footsteps. I whisked Eliza the rest of the way into the office and kneeled down in a dark corner.

"Shh," I said.

"Ssss," she said back.

My knees hit something slimy and squishy that smelled like breakfast. Actually, they hit a whole pile of squishy stuff. I reached down and found myself holding the peel of a recently eaten banana, just as the footsteps went by the office. First one set, and then—another.

Nanny X hadn't mentioned two operatives; she'd said there would be one. Maybe the food stains were wrong! Maybe Nanny X had grabbed Jake and the two of them had managed to escape! But I'd been hearing Jake's footsteps most of my life; these didn't sound like them. And whoever was running down the hall was wearing tennis shoes, not pilgrim shoes.

The footsteps stopped at what had to be the men's bathroom. I heard the door open. Then close.

"Ssss?" Eliza asked me.

"Sneak attack," I told her. "Let's go."

Quietly, so that our feet made barely any noise, Eliza and I made our way toward the bathroom. The door began to open. I pressed myself flat against the wall outside, just in case, as Eliza reached into the diaper bag for another cracker. She came out with a book. "Weed," she said, which is her word for "read."

"No, Eliza," I whispered. "Remember what happened last time." *MOOOOOOOOOOOOOOOOOOOOOOOOOOOOOOOOO.*

The bathroom door opened the rest of the way, and a head poked out—a head I recognized. Only it didn't belong to my brother or Nanny X or Yeti. It didn't even belong to Big Adam. It belonged to—

"Stinky! You're free!" I said.

"Ali! Are you okay?"

He turned back into the bathroom, and his voice echoed: "It's okay, Boris, I found them."

Boris came out of the bathroom, grinning. "Ah," he said. "*Moo, Sweet Cow.* The times we had with that book. Remember, Daniel?"

Stinky put his hands over his ears and nodded.

Wait. They knew about *Moo, Sweet Cow*? That meant the Lentil Nanny must be Nanny X's operative! Okay, I always thought that it was a little strange that Stinky had a male nanny, because he was pretty much the only male nanny I knew. But he'd always taken really good care of Stinky, even if he hadn't fed him very well. He gave better piggyback rides than anyone we knew, and he sang a lot, mostly songs he had learned growing up in Jamaica. I just figured that Stinky's mom had searched extra hard for a male role model, since Stinky's dad wasn't around. Parents do stuff like that.

But if Boris was in NAP, Stinky must have known. And even if he was sworn to secrecy and all of that, he was supposed to be my friend! I would almost have been mad at him, except that we didn't have time if we were going to find my brother and my dog. And Nanny X.

Stinky ran up like he was going to hug me, but he stopped when he was about a foot away and put his hands in his pockets. But Boris grabbed my shoulders. "You are okay then, yes?" he said. He was tall, with wild hair and dark skin. He had a patch of beard just below his lower lip. He looked more like a rock star than a nanny. "You have not been alone long?"

"Not very," I said. I looked at Stinky. "When did you get out?"

"Just a few minutes ago," he said. "I'm on bail, just like on TV. I'm still supposed to appear in court and everything, but they couldn't keep me overnight for—I forget exactly how your mother worded it—something like 'a youth of good standing and tender age accused of committing a minor infraction with less than flimsy circumstantial evidence, no weapon, and no eyewitnesses, this is *total bunk*.' I'm not supposed to leave town, but it's not like my mom would let me go anywhere, anyway; we have school."

School and Ms. Bertram seemed a zillion years away.

I looked at Boris. "You're in NAP?" I asked, no doubt

wowing everybody with those amazing powers of observation I was supposed to have.

"Since Daniel was very small," he said. "Of course, it was much easier to carry the equipment when I had a diaper bag, like yours." He reached toward it. "May I?"

"I guess so."

I handed him the bag, and he began going through it the way Eliza and I had in the bathroom. "Baby powder, excellent. Diapers! How I miss them. I know *you* don't, Daniel, but they were incredibly useful. In more ways than one."

Boris sighed, the way grown-ups do when they're talking about old memories. He handed back the bag and reached for Eliza. She's usually a little shy about going to people she doesn't know well, but Boris bounced her up and down and tickled her under the chin. She tried to grab his tuft of beard.

"So," Boris said. "You two are safe. This is important, yes? But no one has come back? Not your brother? Your nanny? Not the dog?"

"No one." My stomach got that same feeling it got when I was five and got lost at the state fair in Richmond.

Boris put a hand on my head. "Do not worry," he said. "Your nanny is very smart and has excellent training. We will find them in no time. Do you have a tracking device? I'm not sure what is standard issue for nannies with young charges. When Daniel was small, it was a box of Goldfish crackers."

I handed him the bib. The food stains were still in motion.

"Ingenious!" Boris said. "Come. My car's outside." Holding Eliza like she was some sort of golden trophy instead of a toddler with a little bit of drool on her face, he walked out of the building.

*   *   *

It's a good thing there were only four of us, because Boris's car was so small he probably could have given *it* a piggyback ride.

Boris reached into the diaper bag and pulled out the teddy bear. He squeezed its hand. It started to expand, like it was attached to an air pump or something. In seconds it inflated into a car seat for Eliza. He fitted it into the back, and Stinky and I squeezed in next to her.

Boris sat in the front, his long legs bent at an angle that didn't seem good for driving.

"If we hold the bib under this light, we can see a map of Lovett," I said, holding out the pacifier.

"That is one way," Boris said. "Let me try something."

He took the bib and crammed it into a slot just below the CD player. Suddenly colored dots, the same colors as the food stains, appeared on a purple screen in the dashboard.

"When we used Goldfish boxes, we just inserted them in here," he said. "I hoped this might be compatible as well." A monotone female voice called out: *Turn right on Coleman Avenue. Turn left on Watts Street.*

Boris followed the directions, glancing at the purple screen and making predictions. "It looks like they're headed into the District," he said. "No. Wait. Maybe Leesburg?"

Turn right on Wallace Street.

That reminded me of Howard Wallace, who is one of Jake's favorite baseball players. I wondered if my brother was scared. He has the Pringle Stomach, which means he gets kind of nauseous when he's nervous, like my dad. It was a good thing he hadn't eaten anything but radishes.

16. Jake

Nanny X Stays Cool

Here's something I have learned about torture devices: There are the ones on TV, where the bad guys stand around the good guy and shine a light in his face. There are the kinds teachers use, like squeaky chalk and spelling tests. Plus there's the wedgie, which is the type of torture device kids use on each other. And there's the Smoothie Torture. You're probably thinking: Drinking a bunch of free smoothies doesn't sound bad. It sounds *icy*! It sounds *tundra*! Wrong.

The coconut smoothie Big Adam gave me in the van was just the start. He fed me three more smoothies when we got to our destination, an old metal building that I decided was some kind of airplane hangar in the middle of nowhere. He had blenders all over the place. Even the chimp knew how to operate them. He'd waddle up, throw in some coconut guts from the big mound on the table, and press *Blend* with his hairy finger. I didn't think he'd made the coconut loaf or creamed coconut casserole, which Big Adam also fed us. But I could have been wrong.

"Drink!" Big Adam said.

"I can't." I never wanted to see a coconut smoothie—or anything else made out of coconut—again. The pulp kept getting stuck in my throat and making me cough. Then it sloshed around in my stomach, which was already nervous. Nanny X had been forced to drink the smoothies, too, but she was still sitting up straight with her legs tied to the chair next to mine. "Training," she whispered. "With the guy who won the hot-dog-eating contest at Nathan's."

The chimp stood next to us, keeping watch.

"That better be finished by the time I come back," Big Adam said. He stalked off to another part of the hangar. The chimp watched me. His eyes were brown. He didn't look like one of the bad guys. I smiled at him, and he walked over. Yeti, who was tied up on my other side, growled, but not very loudly, as the chimp grabbed my smoothie, stuck the straw in his mouth, and slurped up the rest of it. He handed it back, and smiled and clapped.

"Hey," I whispered. "Thanks, dude."

The chimp clapped again.

People always say there are no bad dogs, only bad owners. Maybe there were no bad chimps, either. Except just then, Mr. Strathmore woke up. Or started to. He moaned on the floor next to us, loud enough for Big Adam to hear.

"Conk him," Big Adam said, coming back toward us. The chimp scooted over to a pile of coconuts and grabbed one off the top. He conked Mr. Strathmore on the head without even blinking. There was another guy on the floor next to Mr. S, too, who was also unconscious. I figured he must be the missing guy from the planning commission. The chimp conked him on the head, too.

"Drink," Big Adam said again. If I did, it meant a mouthful of chimp germs, but I didn't have a choice. I put the straw in my mouth and sucked. The straw filled with air and made a loud, slurping noise.

"I guess it's empty," I said.

"You know what to do," Big Adam told the chimp, who went over to the blender and pushed the button again. Yeti put his head on my foot and lay there. Some rescue dog. He didn't even eat my coconut loaf.

"It was the chimp," Nanny X said over the sound of the blender.

"Hmm?" said Big Adam. He gave us a smile that showed all of his teeth. "What was the chimp?"

"He hit the mayor," Nanny X said during a moment of silence. Then the chimp added some more pieces of coconut and pressed Blend again.

Big Adam went over to the blender and poured another smoothie into my cup. The chimp's eyes were sad, like those baby seals on the poster in the school library.

"Yes," said Big Adam. "Pity. Two targets, and the fuzz ball didn't hit either of them."

"Who was he supposed to hit?" I asked. If I kept him talking, maybe he wouldn't make me drink the next smoothie.

Big Adam looked at the still body of Rufus Strathmore, who was frowning in his sleep. "Him, for one," Big Adam said. "But better late than never."

"But why?" I said. "He was on your side."

"*Sympathy, that's why!*" shouted Big Adam. "If the public saw him fall, they would have to be on the side of business. Someone harmed the business leader! Someone must be against business! All it takes to turn the tide is for the crowd to think you're the underdog. Someone doesn't want business in Lovett, they would say. Poor little business.

Business must be good. That's the way the human mind works. I know a lot about the human mind." He walked over with the smoothie and handed it to me. "I know what it takes to crush it."

"You won't get away with this," Nanny X said, like she'd walked right out of a detective novel.

"I already have," said Big Adam. "In just a few hours, the board will vote in favor of my project. Once something like this gains steam, there's no turning back."

"Two targets," I said. "You said there were *two* targets. One was Mr. Strathmore. Who was the other one?" Maybe Big Adam knew Nanny X was more than a regular nanny. Maybe *she* was the target.

But Nanny X said quietly, "It was the boy."

"Me?" I said.

"Not you, Jake Z," she said. "Daniel."

"Stinky?"

"He was in the crowd," Big Adam said. "No one would have seen it happen. He would have just quietly crumpled to the ground, and he wouldn't have been able to hold up that annoying sign and continue that annoying chant."

"Slides are cool," I said. "Slides are cool!"

"Yes," said Big Adam, wrinkling his nose. "He got the crowd going. If we had made the sign disappear, the sound would have stopped. Well, it stopped anyway, didn't it? All in all, a successful day. Now *drink.*"

I wondered if the coconut smoothies had some sort of chemical in them that would hypnotize me into believing Big Adam was a good guy. Nope. I still knew he was bad. B.A.D.

The chimp looked at me with those brown eyes again, and I knew he would take that smoothie off my hands if Big Adam would just turn his back. But he didn't.

We were stuck in the hangar until the vote, at least. But what if it didn't go his way? What would he do with us then? And what if it *did* go his way? How could he release us, knowing what we knew? Maybe he'd erase our memories to keep us from talking. Maybe coconuts worked on your memory and—

"When you don't return home this evening, people will think you disappeared from the park," Big Adam said. "They'll think public parks are dangerous and that I'm doing everyone a favor by replacing it with my little 'business.'"

Something about the way he said "business" didn't feel right, but then, nothing Big Adam said felt right. But he was forgetting one thing: Ali and Eliza were still out there. Ali would tell everybody where we *really* were when we disappeared. Unless somebody had gotten to her, too.

"Drink," Big Adam said for the kazillionth time. The chimp looked at me as if to say *I tried,* and shrugged. I took another sip of smoothie, my stomach feeling like it was full of rocks instead of coconuts. Out of the corner of my eye, I saw the flower on Nanny X's hat move. It could have been the wind, only there wasn't any wind in the hangar.

The rocks moved up from my stomach to my chest, kind of like lava, except not as hot.

Even if I wanted to be polite, it was impossible. There was only one thing left to do: *BUUUUUUUUUUUUUUUUUU UUUURRRRRRRRRRRRRRRRRRRRRPPPP.*

17. Alison

Nanny X Is a Bit Hung Up

You know how you can recognize someone's voice? Well, I recognized my brother's burp, right through the walls of the airplane hangar.

"That's Jake," I told Boris and Stinky. "They're in there."

"Then we have to get in there, too," Boris said. He put his ear against the cold metal wall. I did the same. We could hear voices, although nothing was as distinct as my brother's burp. There was a mumble that sounded like Nanny X, and a mumble that was definitely Jake. And then there was another mumble that sounded like "bwahahaha," which had to be Big Adam.

"What is he doing to them?" I asked, not that I wanted an answer.

"They're going to be okay," Stinky said.

"Es!" Eliza seemed to agree with Stinky. I wished I could be that calm.

We pressed our ears to the side of the building again, and this time we heard an "eee eeee" sound—the same sound we had heard through the sippy cup. If only someone hadn't stomped on the teething biscuit, we could use it again and really hear what was going on.

"At least we know Big Adam is working alone," Boris said.

"No," I said. I remembered where I'd heard that "eee eeee" sound before. And those bananas in Mr. Strathmore's office? They weren't just there by coincidence. "He has a partner. This is going to sound crazy, but I think he's working with a monkey."

Boris smiled. "In the spy biz, we call them rats, not monkeys, Alison," he said.

"No," I said. "He's working with a *real* monkey. Eliza and I found banana peels everywhere, and that 'eee eeee' sound we keep hearing—I'm sure it's a monkey."

"The rock," remembered Stinky. "Or the coconut or whatever. A monkey could have thrown it."

"A real monkey?" Boris repeated. "Now things are beginning to make sense, no?" When he said "things" it sounded more like "tings." "I'm going in. Let's see if Big Adam can handle a NAP attack. Wait for my signal; I'll let you know when it's clear."

"Can't we come, too?" I said. I sounded like a whiny kid.

But Boris chose that moment to hand me Eliza. I got his point right away: It was safer if he went first. He was in NAP. And Stinky and Eliza and I, we were just the cover. We were the reason he got to carry around a bunch of explosives in a diaper bag.

"Wish me luck," Boris said. He and Stinky did a handshake thing that ended with their thumbs pointing upward. Maybe Nanny X would teach us a secret handshake, too. If we got out of this.

I wondered if Nanny X would even want to stay out the week. I hadn't been exactly nice to her since she started working with us. I'd yelled at her for letting Big Adam take Jake, and she'd given herself up to be with him. And Jake—he wouldn't have been caught in the first place if I hadn't fallen when I was trying to climb up the bathroom walls. It was *my* fault my brother and Nanny X and Yeti were all locked in that hangar. And I hadn't even gotten any valuable information—all I'd seen over the stall was Big Adam rattling around with two coconut halves. Two perfect halves.

But wait.

Maybe that *was* important. He hadn't been trying to take the coconut apart when I saw him. He'd been trying to put the pieces together. And what else had I seen? Not milk, not the white coconut flesh, but the glimmer of something shiny. "In the bathroom," I told Boris, "I saw Big Adam with two parts of the coconut. He was fitting them together. Like those plastic Easter eggs."

"A hiding place?" Boris guessed.

"I didn't get a good look at what he was hiding in there," I said. "But yeah."

Boris took the bib, which he'd ejected from the car dashboard, and handed it to Stinky. "If I'm not out in seventeen minutes, you will contact the police, yes? Give them these coordinates. They'll come." He handed the diaper bag to me. "Eliza may need a change." He cracked open the side door of the airplane hangar, and slid inside.

I jiggled Eliza up and down. Stinky looked like he'd been through this before. Lots of times.

"So how'd you get out of jail?" I said.

"That call from your mother. After she told them that thing she told them, she faxed them a letter. And she called the judge. And she mentioned a lawsuit. But she also said I wasn't a flight risk and the nearest detention center was in Lorton, and couldn't they just release me to my mother and Boris? Then the judge talked to me and I told her what you said, about how I couldn't have thrown anything because my hands were full. She seemed to believe me. She didn't drop the case because the mayor didn't drop the charges, but she thought it was okay to let me out on bail."

"How much?" I asked, putting Eliza on the ground. She picked up a stick and banged it. I was afraid she was going to poke her eye out, but even that seemed safer than handing her something from the diaper bag.

"Eight thousand dollars."

"Whoa." I had never known anyone worth eight thousand dollars before. But I was still mad at him for keeping his secret for so long.

"You always complained about Boris," I said. "All of those lentils."

"Yeah, well, if you had to eat as many lentils as I eat, you'd complain, too," said Stinky.

"You mean the lentils weren't just a part of his cover?"

"I wish."

"Why didn't you tell me about him? About *you*?"

"It was a secret," he said.

"Well, why didn't you tell me after you saw Nanny X? You knew she was in NAP, didn't you, when you saw her at the park?"

"I suspected. But I was a little busy *being arrested*, remember? And you were only supposed to find out when your nanny thought you were ready." Stinky looked at me and smiled. "I guess she decided you were ready pretty quick. Boris didn't decide I was ready for two and a half years."

"Yeah, but you were like three years old when your mom hired him," I said. Still, I grinned back. "Where was he, anyway? While you were at the park?"

"He was checking out a pickup truck that was parked in the cul-de-sac. Someone stole some diamond necklaces from Bell's Jewelers this morning, and Mrs. Bell said they got away in a red truck. My mom's really mad he wasn't with me, but it wasn't all Boris's fault. I'm allowed to go to the park by myself, usually."

"They may not let you anymore," I said.

Just then, a truck turned down the road and the three of us scrambled to the other side of a small hill, flattening our stomachs against it.

"That's the same truck that was parked near our house," Stinky whispered. "I know it is."

The doors opened, then slammed, and we peeped over the hill to see what was going on. Two men got out. But that wasn't all.

"Boris was *totally* wrong about Big Adam working alone," I said. And I was wrong about the monkey. First because it wasn't a monkey; it was a chimp. And second because it wasn't one chimp; it was about twenty of them—enough to eat all of the bananas at Nolan's Market. Enough to do some serious damage if they were under the control of an evil bad guy. Big Adam's partners got them into formation, and they started marching toward the airplane hangar. They opened the door that Boris had sneaked through, and stepped inside, two by two.

I looked in the diaper bag to see if there was anything that could help us. But there were no baby objects labeled Press Here in Case of Chimp Attack.

"Has it been seventeen minutes yet?" I asked. Something in the diaper bag must have doubled as a stopwatch. But what? The pacifiers? *Moo, Sweet Cow*?

And worse than that: How were we supposed to even call the police if seventeen minutes had passed? I didn't have my own cell phone—I wasn't getting one until I started middle school. Stinky didn't have a phone, either. Which meant that we had only one form of communication left, and I wasn't sure how to use it: Nanny X's exploding diaper.

18. Jake

Nanny X Springs Into Action

Big Adam stood in front of us with his blender.

Behind him, I noticed something moving in the shadows near one of the doors to the outside. Boris! Stinky's nanny! Nanny X must have seen him, too. I could tell by the way she tried to keep Big Adam focused on us.

N.A.P. Nanny Action Patrol. I guessed Boris was a member, too. He seemed like he was pretty good at the secret-agent stuff. He made it halfway across the room without Big Adam seeing him. Three-quarters of the way. He had almost reached Big Adam when the door to the hangar opened and two huge men walked in. It didn't look like they were on our side.

"Oy!" one of them said.

Big Adam turned toward the voice, and of course he saw Boris. The two men went charging toward Stinky's nanny. They were followed by a whole army of chimps. I had named the smoothie chimp Howard after Howard Wallace, my favorite baseball player. If I was stuck there long enough, I would have to come up with names for the new chimps, too. And it looked like we were going to be stuck: The men, who were Big Adam's assistants, I guess, tied Boris to a chair like the rest of us. Boris didn't look worried, though. He looked almost happy.

He caught Nanny X's eye and gave her a wink, the *Don't worry* kind.

The new chimps weren't as nice as Howard. When they started screaming "*eeee chee chee*" it didn't sound like they were making conversation; it sounded like they were out for blood.

Big Adam stood in front of Boris. "Who are you?" he said. "How did you get here?"

Boris didn't answer.

He just sat there looking happy and mysterious, which made Big Adam crazy.

Finally Big Adam gave up, and he and his two assistants started loading some coconuts into the back of his small, orange plane. That's when Ali came in, carrying my little sister. She hadn't gone home and taken the Keep Out sign off her door. She'd tried to find me. She *had* found me. Stinky was with her, too. On the bright side, if he was free, that meant we'd successfully completed one of our missions. But there was a bad side, too, because he was about to be trapped by somebody else.

Ali ran straight for me with Eliza, who was carrying a giant stick and waving it around like she was getting ready to hit a home run, or at least a double. She was still waving it when Alison set her on the ground and began to untie me. "Doofus," she whispered. But she didn't say it like the new, keep-out Ali; she said it like the old Ali, the one who was ready to do something fun or crazy and thought it was okay for me to come along. The one who was not a Super Snot.

"Well, well," called Big Adam, because unfortunately, Ali wasn't invisible. "Who do we have here? Really, Nanny Dearest, you've brought me such delightful company today."

"That's enough, Adam," said Nanny X. "The game's up."

"That's right," Boris said. "Even as we speak, dozens of police officers are on their way to this very hangar. They have our coordinates."

He smiled and nodded at Ali, who got that same look she gets when our mother asks her if she's remembered to put out the recycling. She leaned over and whispered something to Nanny X, who whispered back and gave her a small smile.

Big Adam shook his head and made a *tsk-tsk* noise.

"The police," Big Adam said. "*Please.* The girl hasn't called them. And even if she has, we'll be gone long before they arrive." He spun the propeller on his plane.

"*Seize them!*" he yelled. The chimps surrounded us. A few of the bigger ones moved in on Ali and Eliza.

"No," I said, standing up, since Ali had undone all of my knots. "Leave us alone."

The chimps ignored me.

Then, all of a sudden, I heard a shriek. It was Howard. "*Eeee,*" he said. "*Eee-ee-ee.*"

The chimps stopped moving forward. They looked at my sisters. They looked at Stinky. They looked back at Howard.

"*Eee,*" Howard said again.

And then the chimps backed away. They climbed on top of a pile of coconuts and clapped their hands, like they were watching a play. Howard followed them.

"Seize them or I'm cutting you off," Big Adam said. "No

more bananas. No more coconuts. I'm cutting you off, I'm telling you."

But the chimps just kept sitting and clapping. Howard looked over at Big Adam and blew him a giant raspberry.

Big Adam turned to one of his assistants. I nicknamed them the Rhinos because that's what they looked like charging across the room that first time. Plus, the place was already kind of like a zoo, with all of those chimps.

"Get 'em, Francis," Big Adam said.

The Rhino charged. But Stinky charged, too. He ran straight at Francis like a kid who had been falsely accused of a crime, handcuffed, stuck in a tiny room at the police station, and gotten his geode taken away as evidence, and was really, really ticked off about it. While Stinky charged, Ali used her knot-untying skills to free Nanny X, Yeti, and Boris.

"The bag! The bag!" said Nanny X. "Quickly."

Ali slid the diaper bag toward her, and Nanny X pulled out a diaper—*the* diaper. She handed it to Yeti as if it were a bone.

"Airplane, Yeti," she said. "Airplane. Go."

Yeti stood there with the diaper in his mouth and looked at me. I wasn't sure what Nanny X had in mind, but I was glad she had some sort of plan. "Go on, Yeti!" I said, pointing at the plane. "You can do it."

Just then Mr. Strathmore created a diversion (another reading connection word) by regaining consciousness. "You won't get away with this, Adam," he said.

"Oh, but I already have," said Big Adam. He lifted another crate of coconuts and looked at Mr. Strathmore, just as Yeti dropped the diaper inside the open door of the plane.

"I should have known you couldn't be trusted," Mr.

Strathmore said. "I don't even like coconuts. But all I saw was money."

Big Adam smiled. "We're not so different, you know," he said. "That coconut was meant for you, by the way. Hitting my close friend the mayor was a mistake. But it worked out for the best. Because now they're blaming him." He took one hand off the crate and pointed at Stinky, who was stuck in an armlock with Francis.

"Personally, I never cared for coconuts, either," Big Adam said, moving toward the cargo hold of the plane. "But I've acquired a taste for them because I like their shells. Oh yes, I *do* like their shells."

"Smuggling," Boris called, as Ali finished untying his feet.

"I prefer the term 'distribution,'" said Big Adam. "And right now I'm going to be distributing a few things to my private island."

"Diamonds," guessed Nanny X.

"You catch on fast," said Big Adam. "Not that it will do you any good. I think it's time to distribute *you* to my private island as well. I'm sure you'll manage very well there. I recently acquired a geologist who is aiding in my mineral operations. Mr. Snavely could use some help. I hope you like spiders. The island is full of them."

I guess Mr. Strathmore didn't like spiders; he looked like he had the willies.

Francis the Rhino got Stinky in a headlock with one arm, and picked up a coconut with the other. He aimed it right at our nanny's head.

"No, you imbecile, not *that* coconut!" Big Adam yelled. His face looked pale, like coconut milk. But Francis had already started his windup. I grabbed the stick out of

Eliza's hand and stood in front of Nanny X. I choked up as the coconut came hurtling toward us. *Whack.* The coconut soared through the air and landed at Big Adam's feet. The two halves split apart, and small, shiny things spilled out. They scattered on the floor like frozen tears. Diamonds! My Fantastically Freaky book says that some diamonds came to the Earth in meteorites, but it doesn't say anything about coconuts. My new secret-agent brain told me that these were the stolen Gudula diamonds, and that the person who had stolen them was Big Adam.

Eliza crawled over and picked up a diamond like it was a raisin. "Pity," she said. It sounded like she felt sorry for Big Adam, but I am pretty sure that was just her word for "pretty."

"*Those are mine!*" Big Adam yelled. His face turned the color of a strawberry, and I wondered if he had a button on him someplace, because he looked like he was about to explode.

19. Alison

Nanny X's Bag of Tricks

Nanny X opened up the diaper bag.

"Boris, children: Choose your weapons," she said.

Boris grabbed the copy of *Moo, Sweet Cow.* "For old times' sake," he said.

Nanny X grabbed a jar of beef-and-gravy baby food.

"What do these do?" asked Jake, grabbing a bunch of yellow pacifiers, the ones that were labeled Stinky Binky.

"Stink bombs," Nanny X explained. Jake handed some to me.

Stinky, of course, was still doing the tango with Francis, so he didn't grab anything, even though the pacifiers sort of had his name on them.

"Now," said Nanny X, "squeeze and heave."

I squeezed the bulb of the pacifier, and right away smoke started pouring out. I threw it toward Big Adam. Soon the room smelled like hard-boiled eggs. Really old hard-boiled eggs. Which was disgusting but made me kind of hungry at the same time.

Jake threw his pacifier, aiming for Stinky and Francis. I hoped Stinky could get at least one hand free so he could hold his nose. But then, he was used to bad smells.

Big Adam's other assistant came charging toward us, and Nanny X turned to face him. "Untie Mr. Strathmore and his friend," she told us. "I've got this." She opened the jar of baby food. It looked like ground-up erasers. Then she crouched, the way a tiger crouches—or a special agent— and pulled a small metal spoon from her gardening hat.

"Back off," she said. "Or else." The man slowed his advance, but he didn't stop.

Meanwhile, I studied the knot that was holding Mr. Strathmore's wrists. It was actually a series of knots—a square knot on top of a granny knot and then another square knot. But the rope was pulled tight and my fingernails were too short to get in there, from biting them. I pulled a barrette out of my hair and started prying apart the bits of rope.

"Thank you," he said. "Miss . . ."

"Alison," I said.

"Thank you, Alison," said Mr. Strathmore. "I didn't fancy getting sent to an island in the Pacific. I love it in Lovett!"

I closed my eyes so I could focus all of my powers of persuasion right on Mr. Strathmore. Then I opened my eyes, and I opened my mouth up, too. "You won't love it in Lovett for very long if you let people clog up the park with a bunch of factories," I said.

"You don't understand the complexities," Mr. Strathmore said. I had worked through the first two knots and was starting on the third. "Not that I support this particular business anymore, but there might be others—"

"Our park doesn't make anybody cough." I interrupted him, even though I'm not supposed to interrupt. I talked fast. "Don't you think the park's pretty?"

"Of course," he said.

"Don't you think the kids need a place to play?"

"Well of course I do."

"Do you know what I think?" I asked as I undid the last knot.

Mr. Strathmore looked me square in the eye, the way grown-ups look at other grown-ups. "What?"

"I think you should give the factories a park of their own and leave Blue Slide Park alone." I didn't mean for it to rhyme, but it did. I pulled out the bib and the Blazing Binky and showed him, in the purple light, a spot in Lovett where there was an empty lot beside a factory that made potato chips.

"That," he said, rubbing his chin now that his hands were completely untied, "is a thought."

"I agree," said the man beside Mr. Strathmore, who was waking up now, too. He held out his hands so I could untie them next. "You," he said to me, "should run for a seat on the planning commission."

Mr. Strathmore was still rubbing his chin when Nanny X scooped up a spoonful of baby food and flicked it at Big Adam's assistant. Somewhere during its flight, the baby food turned into something resembling concrete. Or maybe beef-and-gravy baby food is always that way. It hit Big Adam's assistant in the neck, and he went down.

Which left Francis and Big Adam.

And that's when Boris opened *Moo, Sweet Cow*.

MOOOOOOOOOOOOOOOOOOOOOOOOOOOOOOOOOOOOOO OOOOO.

That cow was even louder in the airplane hangar.

The chimps covered their ears. Yeti tried to cover his, but couldn't. His yelps filled the air along with the moo.

Eliza covered her ears, and so did Francis. Stinky, apparently, had heard the moo enough times in his life that it didn't bother him anymore. He just held his nose and ran toward us.

I was so busy holding my ears that I didn't notice Eliza crawling away from me. When I looked up she was headed straight for the airplane, which was the most dangerous place to be.

"*Eliza, no!*" I yelled. She stopped.

"Come back here, Eliza. *Eliza!* What are you doing?"

But I knew what she was doing, because it was the same thing she did every time my mother had someone important over: She was taking off her diaper. That's why we try to dress her in as many clothes as possible. But apparently Nanny X hadn't used her investigating skills to figure that out. She had put Eliza in a cute little dress. Now here she was, half-naked in a room full of dangerous criminals.

"Gah!" said Eliza. She held the diaper in front of her like a rubber chicken. Then she threw it. She looked very pleased with herself. Yeti whimpered again.

I ran to my sister and snatched her up, hoping she wouldn't pee on me. Then I ran back across the room, away from the plane, and just in time.

There was a thunderous boom as the other diaper— Nanny X's diaper—exploded.

The plane's window was coated with a white, jelly-like substance, like a weird mixture of ant eggs and Vaseline.

"He won't be going anywhere for a while," Nanny X said.

But Big Adam didn't seem to know that. He headed for the front of the plane, making his way through the hard-boiled-egg smoke, covering his ears against the moo, which was getting quieter now.

Then—*shweeeeee*—there was a whizzing sound. Big Adam skidded across the floor, flapping his arms for balance. For a second, it looked like he was trying to fly. But he didn't. Almost as if he was in slow motion, Big Adam started to fall, lower and lower, until he crashed onto the concrete floor of the airplane hangar.

The stink bombs hadn't stopped Big Adam.

Moo, Sweet Cow hadn't stopped him.

But Eliza's diaper—her real diaper—had.

"Eliza!" I said, squeezing her. "You're a hero!"

The chimps stood up on their coconut pile and clapped some more.

My brother walked over to the one wearing the red bandana and shook his hand. "Thanks, Howard," he said.

20. Jake

Nanny X Lets Go of Her Hat

By the time the police arrived, we had tied up Big Adam and his friends. Ali used some of her complicated knots, including one that circled around their legs, so they looked like those people in movies who are tied up on train tracks. I helped with the regular kind. She said she'd teach me some of the fancy ones later, when we got home.

Chief Grummel came in. Stinky stood there giving him looks that were a little mean and a little worried, while Nanny X and Boris showed him the blueprints for a factory that would have made Lovett the Smuggling Capital of the Mid-Atlantic. I don't think the mayor or Mr. Strathmore would have liked that slogan very much. They also showed the chief the diamonds. I'd wanted to open some of the other coconuts to see if we could find even more diamonds, like the ones that had been stolen from Mrs. Bell, but Nanny X didn't want us touching anything, in case of fingerprints. She was sure they'd find more, though.

There was a lot of reading of rights and some blah blah blah about what would happen to the diamonds and whether the mayor should be forced to leave office, but I didn't care about any of that stuff. "What's going to happen to them?" I said. I meant the chimps, who weren't clapping anymore. They were wearing their sad faces, like they'd just found out there really was a banana shortage.

"We'll have to call animal control," said Chief Grummel. "Looks like they'll need backup."

Stinky had a different answer. He looked at me and Ali. "We saved the park," he said. "And you saved me. So now I guess that means it's time to . . ."

"*Save the chimps!*" we all said together.

"Save the chimps," Stinky agreed. "I'll make a sign: Chimps Are Cool."

"*Tundra* cool," I said.

"I'll have a talk with the mayor," Ali volunteered.

"Why not?" said Nanny X. "I think he owes us one—as long as he's still in office."

Several phone conversations later, the authorities (that's a TV word, not a reading connection word) promised to send the chimps to the David T. Jones Sanctuary for Wayward Primates. We went with them as far as the police station, where they waited in a cell with a lot of bananas for the sanctuary people to show up.

I was hoping we could keep Howard, especially since Yeti wasn't barking at him anymore and Yeti didn't do that for just anyone. But Nanny X said no.

"They were meant to be wild," she said. "He'll be happy at the sanctuary. You'll see."

But our nanny looked sad, too. Howard reached up and grabbed her crazy gardening hat and put it on his own head.

"Eee ee!" he said.

He was still wearing the hat when the sanctuary people came to take him away.

"He can keep it," Nanny X said. "It looks better on him, anyway."

Howard looked back at us and waved, and every single one of us waved back, including Chief Grummel but especially me.

"Have fun," I said. "Don't drink too many coconut smoothies."

One of the sanctuary people reached for Howard's hand, and he took it. I wiped my eyes, in case of crying. I thought about Howard swinging from the trees. I thought about Howard in a place where nobody was going to call him a hair ball anymore. And all of a sudden I stopped being sad, and it wasn't just because I thought he'd have a good time at the David T. Jones Sanctuary for Wayward Primates; it was because somehow I knew I would see that chimp again someday.

21. Alison

Nanny X Calls It a Day

After my brother cried like crazy over those chimps, and after the sanctuary people drove off in their van, Nanny X said we had to be going, too.

Mr. Strathmore stopped us on the way out.

"I want you to know," he said in his very businesslike voice, "I've taken your ideas into account, and I'm going to talk to the mayor about canceling tonight's zoning hearing. There's no need to hurry, now that Big Adam's business plan is off the table, and I think we have a lot more to think about. I also think we need to leave Blue Slide Park as it is."

We cheered, and Mr. Strathmore cleared his throat and went on.

"Also, I think creating a park for industry is a wonderful idea. It will allow us to keep moving forward, while keeping the things we love about our town the same. After all—we love it in Lovett!"

Mayor Osbourne, who showed up at the police station

at the same time we did, said something about Applesauce King, an environmentally friendly applesauce company, but nobody was listening to him anymore. As we left the police station we passed the lady from the protest, who said she'd just heard there was a possible opening for the position of mayor and she would like to be considered for the job.

Stinky gave her the thumbs-up sign. Mayor Osbourne did not.

"We'd better get going," Boris said, putting a hand on Stinky's shoulder. "I don't want to get in trouble with your mother two times in the same day."

"Wait," Stinky said. He held up something round that looked nothing like a coconut. "Look what Chief Grummel gave me: I got my rock back."

"Is it a real geode?" Jake asked.

"I don't know yet."

Nanny X reached into the diaper bag and pulled out what looked like a set of nail clippers. But it had other attachments, too; one of them was a hammer.

"Perfectly balanced," she said, handing it to him.

Stinky put the rock on the sidewalk outside the police station and gave it one good crack. The rock split. Inside, it resembled one of Big Adam's coconuts—one that had been filled with diamonds.

"Quartz," Stinky said. "It's a good one!"

He handed me one of the halves. If you held it a certain way, it looked like a glass castle.

"It's really beautiful," I said.

"I want you to have it," said Stinky. He picked up the other half and gave it to Jake.

"Thanks," we said.

"You're welcome," said Stinky. He looked at Eliza. "I'm sorry there weren't more pieces," he said.

"She would have just tried to eat it, anyway," I said. "When she's older, she can share mine."

We walked together until we reached the corner of Hummel Street, where it was time to part ways.

"Come," Boris said. "I'll make you dinner."

"Please, can we have something other than lentils?" Stinky asked.

Boris smiled. "You've been through an ordeal today," he said. "Tonight I will make my special jerk chicken."

For Stinky, that was as good as a happily ever after.

"See you," I said.

"See you," Stinky said.

He paused and got all serious. I thought for a minute he might even say something mushy. Instead he said: "Don't forget to recycle."

"You, too."

Then we all got the giggles, and we would have kept on giggling except Nanny X said we had to get out of there lickety-split because we needed to finish our schoolwork before our parents came home.

Even at Nanny X speed, we were behind. "You do your homework. I'll make the dinner. Your parents will be here in twenty-seven minutes."

"We're not having lentils, are we?" I asked, just to make sure Boris hadn't rubbed off on her.

"Or anchovies?" Jake added.

Nanny X smiled. "How about spaghetti and meatballs?"

Jake and I nodded, though I wasn't sure how he could eat anything after all of those coconut smoothies.

"Good," she said. "Now go."

Jake and I ran upstairs and did the rest of our homework. We were back in the kitchen by 6:33.

"I'll set the table!" I said.

"I'll help!" said Jake.

"I knew I could count on you." Something about the way Nanny X looked at us made me think she was talking about a lot more than just getting ready for dinner. She smiled again, a big, bright smile that lit up her whole face. I smiled back.

At 6:42 on the nose our parents walked into the house.

I ran up and gave them both a giant hug before they even made it out of the hallway. So did Jake. Eliza grabbed their knees and looked up at all of us. "Mamamamamama-mama," she said.

"That's some greeting," my father said.

"You'll be happy to know that your friend Daniel is out of jail," my mother said. "Of all the ridiculous—arresting a child. I don't know what kind of power-hungry—but it did make for an interesting first day of work. How was your day?"

"Interesting," I said.

"Tundra," said Jake.

Nanny X came to the doorway of the kitchen. If you didn't know better, you'd have thought she was a regular nanny. "Well," she said. "If you won't be needing me anymore, I'll be on my way."

My father sniffed the air and followed his nose into the kitchen, and my mother followed him.

"We do need you!" Jake said.

Nanny X looked at him, and then at me. I nodded. So did she. Because the thing is: I think Nanny X needed us, too.

I wanted to ask if she was scared when Big Adam tied her up.

I wanted to ask how she knew the diaper would explode at just the right moment, and if she and Boris had ever worked together before, and if she knew that Jake and I would be able to figure out all of the things we'd figured out, and what kind of a hat she was going to get next.

But mostly I wanted to know if Nanny X was coming back.

"Get plenty of rest tonight," she said as she grabbed her motorcycle jacket. "You never know what tomorrow may bring."

She picked up her diaper bag and slung it over her shoulder. Jake and I followed her onto the porch and watched her walk out into the evening.

"Kids!" our mother yelled from the kitchen. "Come sit down to dinner. I want to tell you all about my new job."

"I want to tell you about mine," I said quietly, more to Jake than to her. He looked at me and grinned. The two of us stood at the door long enough to watch Nanny X climb into her minivan. She waved at us through a pair of fuzzy dice that were hanging from her mirror, and gunned the motor twice.

"We forgot to talk to her about being inconspicuous," Jake said.

"We'll talk to her about it tomorrow," I told him. "She's coming back tomorrow."

Then we both went inside to eat our spaghetti before it got cold.

How to Play Breakfast Cereal Baseball
By Jake Pringle

1. Buy some breakfast cereal. Round is best.

2. Fill bowl with milk and put it on one side of the table.

3. Sit down on the *other* side of the table. Using your fingers, flick balls of cereal toward milk.

4. If ball lands on table, it's a base hit. If ball lands on floor, it's a foul. If ball lands in milk, it's a home run.

5. Three foul balls equal one out.

6. If ball hits dad or sisters, it equals one out.

7. If ball hits mom or nanny, it equals two outs.

8. Don't forget to clean up foul balls, or else you might never play again.

Nanny X's Recipe for Peanut Butter and Anchovy Sandwiches

Use two slices of bread—whole grain preferred.

Slather one side with peanut butter.

Place five to six anchovies directly on the peanut butter.

Voilà! Lunch is served!

Please note: One tablespoon of peanut butter should have about 4 grams of protein. Each anchovy provides 1 extra gram of protein.

How to Stop Biting Your Nails
By Alison Pringle

1. Paint your nails a super dark color so that everyone can see if you're biting them.

2. Wear gloves. (I should have tried this in January instead of spring.)

3. Wear socks on your hands at night. (January is best for this, too.)

4. Hot pepper.

5. Pick a nail, like your pinky, to be your "safe nail," but keep biting the others. At the end of the week, add another safe nail, and so on.

6. Tie knots.

7. Tie more knots.

8. Wear bandages on all of your fingers.

Note: This makes it difficult to tie knots. It makes it even more difficult to untie them.

Big Adam's Recipe for Coconut Smoothies

Start out with about 2 ounces of coconut meat, fresh or frozen.

Add ⅓ cup milk, 5 tablespoons coconut cream, ¼ cup sweetened condensed milk, and ¼ teaspoon vanilla.*

Add three or four ice cubes and blend until smooth.**
Makes 1 large serving.

*Fresh ingredients may not be immediately available if you happen to be confined in the federal prison system.

**Blenders may not be available, either.